Cheaters Never Win

DEB GEARHART

Fulton Books, Inc.
Meadville, PA

Published by Fulton Books 2021

ISBN 978-1-63710-934-2 (paperback)
ISBN 978-1-63710-935-9 (digital)

Printed in the United States of America

I would like to dedicate this book to my husband, Jerry, who has supported me in every endeavor over the years.

I would like to recognize all my friends and colleagues at Penn State, Dakota State University, Troy University, Ohio University, the University of South Dakota, who always supported me and provided the inspirations for this novel.

Prologue

The soldier drove past the house several times, trying to figure out the best point of entry to enter unseen. She slides her car into a parking place across the street from the house to observe the activity around the house and around the neighborhood. This is a beautiful neighborhood in an old section of Birmingham. The one-hundred-plus-year-old majestic homes lined the street with huge oaks covered in Spanish moss adorning the street between the sidewalk and the curb. Looking around this historic and expensive neighborhood stirred the ire in Pvt. Emily Stone. Her online instructor lives in that huge white house with the columns out front and the huge veranda. She was so angry with her, with Dr. Gloria Benson, for the failing grade she had received in her online biology course and…for getting Stone suspended from the online associate degree program she was enrolled in. The flurry of angry emails to Dr. Benson didn't help Pvt. Stone's situation, nor did the threats. Now Emily Stone will never get in the cybersecurity program she wanted; the only thing she was working for, what she lived for. Well, now it's time to make good on those threats. Dr. Benson cost Emily Stone the chance to receive her associate degree, all because of this biology course.

Pvt. Stone slouched down in the seat of her jet-black Chevy Impala. It was an older car, a 2000, but Emily kept it up and it drove like a dream. Sometimes too smoothly, Emily has had a few speeding tickets. The police were patrolling the neighborhood. That seemed odd for this neighborhood.

"Maybe Dr. Benson complained about those threats after all," Emily said to herself sarcastically.

Dr. Benson said she was going to address the threats with the director of DTI Online at Dakota Technical Institute. Emily was enrolled in the associate degree program at DTI Online, working toward being accepted into the Online Cyber Security Program offered there.

Well, I guess I just need to stake out the house for a while and see how often they come around, thought Emily.

While sitting in her car thinking, "I need this degree," Emily said to herself. *I have too much at stake,* she thought.

Emily Stone joined the army right out of high school. A lot of her friends decided to join the Army National Guard and go to college at the same time. Emily wanted to get the hell out of South Dakota, so she thought she'd go to the army full-time and school part-time.

"I thought I'd have a chance to see the world, hoping maybe to be in Germany or Korea, but I ended up in Augusta [Georgia]," she spat out while she pounded the steering wheel.

Her life wasn't going the way she wanted it to. And now it really is in the crapper. Getting that associate degree was going to finally give her a chance at getting into the cybersecurity program she wanted. It was Emily's goal to work as cybersecurity in the Pentagon.

A couple hours later, Emily was ready to go. She had been studying the house while sitting in her car. The entryway was surrounded by two enormous pillars, about three feet around at the base and narrowing to the porch roof, which was just about as high as the second story of the house; there was a huge white wooden door under the front porch and a pair of wooden rockers enclosing it. The veranda that surrounded the side of the house was decked out with white wicker porch furniture. The garage was around back at the end of a long driveway on the other side of the house.

The patrol car has been cruising by every hour and Emily noticed the lights had all gone out in the house.

After the next time the cop goes by, I'm going to slip around back and check for a way into the house, thought Emily. As she worked through the plan in her mind, she decided she better make killing Dr. Benson quick instead of slow and painful, there won't be time. *I need to get in and out. But Dr. Benson has to pay for ruining my life.*

Just past midnight, the patrol car had driven by. Emily slipped out of her car.

"God, it feels good to stand up and stretch," groaned Emily.

She gracefully glided across the street, then staying in the shadows of the trees, moved around the house to the garage. Without knowing for certain, Emily hoped there was no security system. She suspected the police patrol might be because Dr. Benson doesn't have the security of a system. Emily didn't know if Dr. Benson was even married. For a split second, Emily wondered if this was a good idea, but it was only for a second. Thinking about her situation, Emily was furious all over again; she moved toward the garage window. Emily slipped on a pair of latex gloves and using her KA-BAR, she sliced through the screen and pushed the KA-BAR under the window to see if it would slide up. It did. Emily pulled out the rest of the screen and crawled through the window. She was counting on the windows in the garage not being locked.

"Well look at that," grimaced Emily, "The bitch has a Beamer." Emily took the point of her KA-BAR down the side of the car as she walked toward the inside garage door. "Now let's hope the inside garage door isn't locked either. Most people don't lock their inside garage doors because they think they are secure with the overhead garage door being down and locked."

Emily slowly opened the inside garage door. She pulled the Maglite out of her pocket and scanned around the kitchen. She didn't want to walk into anything.

It was a good thing I did, thought Emily. *I would have walked right into an island with bar stools.*

Emily scanned around the huge kitchen, all nicely remodeled, with every modern kitchen gadget out.

"Benson must like to cook, how domestic!" Then silently she crept her way through the kitchen.

Emily needed to find the stairs. Like many older, turn-of-the-century homes, there was a long wooden hallway to the front of the house and to the staircase. The hallway was covered with family pictures.

So Dr. Benson is married. What a happy looking family. If I didn't need to be so quiet, thought Emily. *I would knock all of these damn happy people off the wall.*

Emily tried to walk as lightly as she could down the hallway as to not make the old wooden floor creak. Dr. Benson and her idyllic and perfect life just made Pvt. Stone more furious.

It's just not fair.

Emily took a moment to scan into the living room that was off to the left of the stairs. It was a beautiful Victorian-style room with a fireplace and huge front windows. It was very tastefully decorated in a way to combine the old-style room with modern furniture and electronics, including a huge flat screen TV above the fireplace mantle. Every step of her way through Dr. Benson's home just made Emily's hatred grow and made her more determined in her plan.

Emily knew Dr. Benson would be upstairs in bed. Slowly and quietly, she crept up the stairs. At the top, Emily paused.

Which bedroom? she thought. *Does she leave the bedroom door open or shut? Will her husband be in bed with her, or is he gone as she suspected? Just look in the first door, it is open.*

Nothing, it was a guest bedroom. Emily tried the next door. Holding her breath, Emily slowly turned the doorknob, hoping it wasn't a squeaky door. She breathed out slowly, it was not. Emily took a quick scan of the room with her Maglite. It was decorated with a quilt and pillows on an armchair and of course, a very expensive bedroom suite. Silently, the army private crept to the bedside as if she was floating. She looked down on her victim. No one else in bed, what luck. Dr. Benson didn't look like what Emily expected. Dr. Benson wasn't the older, dumpy, mean-looking science teacher that she imagined. Gloria Benson was in her late thirties, trim and pretty. Emily hesitated.

No, she thought. *I have come too far. I have invested too much. I have gotten in too deep…*

Emily pulled out her KA-BAR, leaned over Gloria Benson, whispered, "Die, you bitch!" in her ear. And as Gloria Benson opened her eyes, Pvt. Emily Stone slit her throat.

Sunday

Chapter One

Pvt. Emily Stone barely remembered leaving the house and hoped that she didn't leave any telltale signs of herself as she left out the back door.

I wore latex gloves, I should be okay, she thought to herself.

She was in and out in twelve minutes. She started her car and drove off, then she looked at her hands. They were covered in blood. Emily never thought about the blood. She ripped off the latex gloves, but she got blood on her hands. Her steering wheel and inside door were also bloody. The adrenalin rush was more than she expected but really, she just murdered someone. Then it began to sink in, she just *murdered* someone. Panic sets in.

"What am I going to do?" Emily realized she couldn't go back to Fort Gordon. "And I still have unfinished business; I need to head to South Dakota."

But first, she had to get rid of this blood. Emily headed to the nearest convenience store.

Emily thought to herself, *It's a good thing I wore a black long-sleeved shirt. It hides the blood. I'll just walk right into the restroom with my hands in my pockets.*

As she exited the car, she saw blood on the door handle. She wondered if she left blood smears as she left the house but assuring herself that it was okay; she knew she had latex gloves on.

Emily walked into the convenience store with her hands in her pockets. It was nice of the older truck driver to hold the door for her. She thanked him and he nodded back at her. Emily nearly scrubbed her hands raw getting the blood off, as if scrubbing her hands would scrub away what she had just done. Emily thought she better get some coffee for the drive ahead, so she poured a large dark roast and grabbed some doughnuts. She also grabbed some wipes to take care of the car door, inside door, and steering wheel.

After cleaning off the door and inside of the car, Emily drove over to the pumps, topping off the tank of her car and disposing of the bloody wipes in the huge garbage can by the gas pumps. Emily was ready for the long drive to South Dakota. Emily used her phone to find the quickest route to I40.

Chapter Two

Emily Stone grew up on a farm not far from Ramona, South Dakota. She has the typical Scandinavian look, blond hair, blue eyes, about five feet and nine inches. Her athletic form comes from her work on the family farm and playing basketball. Growing up in a small town in South Dakota, you knew everyone and there was always a helping hand in time of need. But growing up in a small town of 180 people was not enough for Emily. That's why Emily didn't want to go to college in South Dakota, she wanted to see more of the country, more of the world than just Ramona, South Dakota. Emily joined the army and was working on her education online with her educational benefits. She wanted to get into the cybersecurity program at Dakota Technical University through DTI Online. So actually, she is going to college in South Dakota.

That all fell apart after DTI Online did their review of the online video of course exams; Emily was caught cheating along with Haley Jorgenson and her group. Emily was going over the whole thing in her mind. Haley Jorgensen worked in student services at DTI Online. She also was enrolled in the same associate degree program as Emily.

"Online courses just aren't as easy as everyone thinks," voiced Emily, for no one to hear, as she drove down the road.

Emily first met Haley in a course discussion board. Many of their posts were similar and they both noticed the similarities. Emily contacted Haley in a course chat and they hit it off. After a bit, they decided to contact each other outside of the course. In their emails and chats, the two discussed similar gripes about instructors, both feeling that their instructors where picking on them. Haley talked about her situation, how she felt about the fact that her supervisor in student services didn't like her and always criticized her work. Haley would work on her course during office hours and thought that was okay, but her supervisor didn't. Haley said that working on her coursework was helping to improve her skills for her job, however her supervisor didn't buy it.

"You might receive tuition assistance to pursue your education, but you are not allowed to work on your courses at work," her supervisor told her.

Emily griped about similar situations, about trying to complete her courses while working at her position as a signal support systems specialist in the US Army Cyber Command. She wasn't going to continue in the field without a better background in cybersecurity. That is why she opted for the cybersecurity degree from DTI Online. However, Emily needed to successfully complete her associate degree first.

Over time, Emily and Haley realized that they were not going to complete many of their courses without some easy way to get good grades. Haley had come up with a way to cheat on the online exams, working with some of the local students. She brought in a few other students, including Emily, by providing them exam questions and answers for a price. Their cheating scheme seemed to be working well until Dr. Benson stopped it.

She's gone now but she was not the only one. I can't go back to Fort Gordon. My life in that field is over now, thought Emily. *I'm going to South Dakota and finish what I started!*

Emily thinks back to the first time she had a course with Colin Kennedy. He seemed like a nice guy on the discussion board and he was willing to be a spokesperson for the class. But Colin turned out to be far from "Mr. Nice Guy" for Emily, Haley, and her group of student friends. Colin turned out to be their downfall. He was the one who figured out what they were doing and how they were cheating and went to Dakota Tech Online about it. Now it's time for payback against Colin.

Students in the online programs at Dakota Tech Online are from all over the country, many of the students are in the military and move all around, including internationally. As with many online programs, the majority of the students live in and around the state where the institution is located. In the case of Dakota Tech, most of the students come from South Dakota, Iowa, and Nebraska.

Colin Kennedy is a typical adult learner, living in South Dakota but unable to attend Dakota Tech full-time on campus. In South Dakota, nearly all students, those full-time at the institutions and those online, rely on financial aid and still must work. That situation is common for students in all states. Even with financial aid, college is cost prohibitive for many Americans. Online programs have grown because of the convenience to be able to keep up with work and family and still work on a college degree. That was the situation for Colin. He lives in the small town of Miller, in central South Dakota. He works at ACE Hardware, is married with two children—a boy and a girl. Colin's goal is to provide a better life for his family. He wants to work in the IT world to do that. The cybersecurity program with Dakota Tech Online was exactly what he was looking for and he takes each course very seriously.

*****

Emily had a long drive ahead of her and lots of time to think. She drove up through Alabama and hit the corner of Memphis and into Arkansas. After crossing into Missouri, heading to I70 to hit I29, Emily started to hit a wall. The adrenalin rush had long ended and Emily knew she had to stop for a while. It's Sunday evening and Emily figured that Dr. Benson's husband had probably found her by now.

"Nobody knows it's me" concluded Emily. "I should be safe for now; I can stop to rest and eat."

So Emily looked for a hotel along I70. She pulled off at a Super 8 with a Denny's nearby. She checked in for the night. Emily walked into the room. It was rather drab. The room could use a coat of paint and the bedspread looked like it was from the 1980s. Emily was too tired to worry about the state of the room.

I need a shower and I need some food, thought Emily.

She took a quick shower but had to put the same clothes on, blood-stained shirt and all. She had not packed for a trip. She had not planned this trip.

"I need to get something to eat before I crash," muttered Emily.

Emily drove over to the Denny's. She walked in at eight o'clock in the evening. The restaurant was rather quiet except for a few truckers. She decided to eat at the counter. Emily ordered the all-American slam with a glass of milk. She passed on coffee as she wanted to sleep. Coffee kept her awake.

When her slam came, she asked the waitress "Where can I buy some clothes? I left in a hurry and didn't pack."

"You take the next left and go three blocks, you'll find a Family Dollar," answered the waitress. "It's closed now but it opens at eight o'clock tomorrow morning."

Emily thanked her and woofed down her meal. As she went to pay, Emily took stock of her cash. She then asked the waitress where the closest ATM was. Set with all the information Emily needed, she headed back to the motel. She stopped at the front desk and asked for a toothbrush and headed to her room. After brushing her teeth, she fell into bed and was sound asleep in minutes.

Monday

Chapter Three

Fall has arrived, the air crisp and cool. It's pheasant season in South Dakota. South Dakota is a state with around 824,235 people and six million pheasants. The semester is in full swing at Dakota Technical Institute. Dakota Technical Institute is located in Bolton, Clay County, South Dakota. Bolton, a small city of 6500, lies along the Missouri River. On the bluff above the city is a closed insane asylum. The bluff is sacred ground for the Sioux, but it had been taken from them. However, after the asylum was established, the Sioux felt the land had become cursed.

When the territory was settled in the late 1880s, a need for an asylum became evident. Many Civil War soldiers moved west and settling new territory was hard on soldiers suffering from what we now know as PTSD. Many families suffered. A doctor from Philadelphia settled in the area and built a huge Victorian-style building on the bluff for the asylum to the dismay of the Sioux. The asylum continued to function for nearly a century, but the asylum had become run down and it was closed in the 1970s with the services moving to a new facility near the local hospital in Yankton.

A few years later, a state senator, a rancher from northwest South Dakota, proposed legislation to award the facility to Dakota Technical Institute. Dakota Tech, like many universities, started out as a normal school preparing teachers. With the growth of technology use in education, the teacher-centered institution had a change in mission to become Dakota Technical Institute, dedicated to advancing technology in education and developing programs to prepare students for technology use in business and industry. The closed asylum was awarded to Dakota Tech along with the responsibility to fund the renovations. Part of the renovation included a Native American museum to be placed in the old Victorian building.

*****

With the semester in full swing, so were the student complaints. Dr. April McKenzie, Director of DTI Online, was busy in her office.

Just another day in paradise, April thought to herself sarcastically.

April McKenzie was sitting at her desk reading emails. Her inbox was full of student complaints about a psychology instructor who hadn't logged into his online course for two weeks. Dr. McKenzie loved working with students but hated when the complaints came in. There was always someone who would be unhappy with her. This meant that in the morning, she needs to contact Professor Johnson and "nicely" remind him that this is only an eight-week online course and he needs to login and provide his students some feedback. That is what he is getting paid to do. Then April would have to contact each of these students to follow-up on their complaints, reassuring them and reinforcing that indeed, their instructor will get back to actively engaging with them. April understands how important time is to these adult learners, but little did she know that one unhappy student was going to take a situation a little too far…leaving April smack dab in the middle of a murder investigation.

April McKenzie is a redhead, about twenty pounds overweight, who has a "bit of a temper." April inherited her red hair from her father who was of Irish descent. Her dad might have given April her red hair, but her redheaded Dad was an even-tempered mill worker. April's temper was all her own. April grew up in a paper mill town in Central Pennsylvania. She had Pennsylvania Dutch roots and at one time thought she'd always live in Pennsylvania. But this opportunity opened in South Dakota and, over time, she came to love the people in South Dakota.

It took April an hour to get an email response from Professor Johnson.

April,

*You emailed me about logging into my course. Sorry
I have been absent; I was at a conference.*

Marc

Marc,

*It would have been helpful if you had let the class
know you would be out of town. You know I stress
that very point in training, being proactive rather
than reactive. You have a number of students who
are unhappy about not having any response on the
last assignment so close to the end of the course.
Colin Kennedy is leading the pack on your open
forum. You need to log in and calm your students
down—and respond to their assignments! This is
happening way too often.*

April

Okay, okay, April. I will catch up today.

Marc.

Thinking the situation would soon be diffused, April responded
to all the students that Professor Johnson would be in touch with
them today.

April McKenzie always knew she wanted to work with people. She had gone to college planning to be a social worker. She had
held several jobs in social services, which she enjoyed, but over time,
April realized working in social services was not for her. She admired
her colleagues who found this work their avocation, but it was not
for her. Thinking back though, April once thought about being an
educator. So she had looked for a position at a local university. It

wasn't too long before April had enrolled into a graduate program and she was on her way to a career in higher education. April landed in a supervisory position in a distance education program and knew right away this is where she wanted to work, helping adult learners achieve their educational dreams. Over the years, she advanced positions in the online learning programs until she ended up at Dakota Technical Institute managing their online program, DTI Online, as the director.

Lori, at the front desk, buzzed April.

"Yes, Lori?" said April, knowing that Lori only buzzed with a problem that she couldn't handle.

Lori told April she better take this call, it was a police detective from Birmingham, Alabama.

April thought to herself, *This can't be good.*

The voice on the phone asked, "Are you Dr. April McKenzie?"

"Yes," April replied. "How may I help you?"

"This is Det. Darius Smiley from the Birmingham PD. Do you have an instructor working for you by the name of Dr. Gloria Benson?"

Det. Darius Smiley was a large African American man. He played football at UAB (the University of Alabama Birmingham) where he had studied criminal justice. April noticed his deep, rich voice which was very soothing.

April responded, "Yes, Gloria teaches biology courses online for our program."

Det. Smiley continued. "I regret to inform you that Dr. Benson was murdered in her home, Saturday night. Her husband was out of town and returned Sunday evening to find her dead in the bedroom."

April gasped. "Oh my god! No!"

Det. Smiley continued, "Mr. Benson mentioned to us that his wife had several student-related issues in her biology course and had worked with you concerning one student in particular who really scared her. Can you tell me about this student? I understand that the department had a patrol detail at their house this weekend while Mr. Benson was out of town."

April was trying to pull herself together. She could not believe what she was hearing.

"Yes, yes, I will try and help you," whispered April. "Please give me a second."

"Of course," responded Det. Smiley.

April took a deep breath and continued. "Dr. Benson had called me about a month ago to discuss some possible cheating on her online exams. We did find a cheating ring that also included a staff member from our office. The staff member was dismissed and the students were suspended. One student has been sending Dr. Benson threatening emails and making threatening calls. I can provide you details."

"That would be great," replied Smiley. "But of more immediacy would be to have the name and contact information for the student who was threatening Dr. Benson."

"Let me grab the file." A couple seconds later, April continued, "She is a student in the army, Pvt. Emily Stone. She is based at Fort Gordon in Augusta, Georgia. I'm not sure whether her contact info is still accurate, but you can contact the base to talk to her. I'm not sure if the army took any action after she was suspended from the program. Would you please provide me your contact information so I can send you the full report on the incident? I need time to digest all of this."

Det. Smiley commented that he understood and provided the contact information, asking to forward the report as soon as possible. He thanked her for her time and hung up.

April sat back in her chair thinking, *What just happened?*

Chapter 4

Meanwhile, back at Fort Gordon, Commander LTG Cook was receiving an update on AWOL Pvt. Emily Stone.

When Emily Stone didn't return to post after killing Dr. Benson, the OIC (Officer in Charge), Lieutenant Franks, called her apartment. It wasn't like Pvt. Stone to not show up for duty. She was so gung ho to work toward her promotion to cybersecurity. However, Lt. Franks had noticed that she wasn't acting like herself the past few weeks. She just didn't seem interested in her work anymore. Now she hasn't shown up for duty and she's not answering her phone. The army, like other the other branches of the military, is now more concerned about suicide within the ranks. Lt. Franks sent another private over to Emily's apartment to see if she was there, to see if there was a problem.

The private returned an hour later and reported to the lieutenant that Pvt. Stone was not at her residence, no one answered the door. He looked in the window and didn't see anything out of place, he noted that her car was not there. Lt. Franks knew he needed to pass this on. Pvt. Emily Stone was nowhere to be found.

By now, LTG Cook was being briefed on the situation. If the servicemember is sick, there are procedures for reporting in that he or she would not be at their post. This clearly was a troubling situation. According to the Lt. Franks, Pvt. Stone has not had been a problematic soldier but there is concern because not only is Pvt. Stone not at her apartment, but her car is not there. The lieutenant knew that Pvt. Stone had been caught in a cheating scheme at Dakota Technical Institute and was suspended from the online cybersecurity program. Not only was Pvt. Stone suspended from her academic program, but she received a reprimand for behavior unbecoming, which also hurt her chances for promotion. He had informed LTG Cook about that situation but also commented that it had not affected her work, maybe her attitude, but not her work. However, LTG Cook knew he had to start the process of reporting Pvt. Stone AWOL.

After the lieutenant left, LTG Cook knew he had a lot to do. He had to notify the personnel office and the provost marshal office. Then there were all the forms that need to be completed and sent to the chief of USADIP (United States Army Deserter Information Point). Mainly, LTG Cook wanted to contact her family to see if they knew where she was, but the NOK of the soldier letter is not sent until the tenth day of AWOL. However, knowing that Pvt. Stone had been out of sorts lately, LTG Cook really wanted to reach out to Pvt. Stone's family to see if they know where she is. Since Pvt. Stone is part of the cybersecurity unit, this could possibly be a national security risk. The situation could be a special category absentee, which would allow him to call Emily's family under 3.3 Special Category. That will include additional forms be completed but from what he heard from the lieutenant, he was concerned this could be a serious situation. It was serious, but not for national security serious.

Once all the paperwork was started and in the proper hands to complete and file, LTG Cook decided to call the Stones. Emily's mother answered the phone.

"Good morning, Mrs. Stone. This is Lieutenant General Cook from Fort Gordon. How are you today?"

Mrs. Stone responded, "Has something happened to Emily?" Mrs. Stone is the typical worrying mother of an active-duty soldier.

LTG Cook continued. "Mrs. Stone, I do not want to alarm you, but I was wondering if you have heard from Emily recently. She did not report for duty today. Her lieutenant had her apartment checked to see if she was sick. She wasn't there and her car is gone."

Carol Stone took a deep breath. "Lieutenant General Cook, we only hear from Emily once a month, if we are lucky, sometimes a month and a half. She seemed in good spirits most of the time. But the last time she called, she was really upset. I asked her about how her courses were going; she is in the online cybersecurity program at Dakota Technical Institute. She was furious after that. She said that 'bitch instructor' in her biology course messed her up big-time. I asked why, but she said she didn't want to talk about it. We have not heard from her since that call. I can't tell you more about why she is upset but please find her. We are worried about her."

LTG Cook spoke with Carol Stone for a few minutes more, reassuring her that they would do all they could to find her daughter. He ended the call by asking Mrs. Stone to please call him if she or any of the family heard from Emily.

LTG Cook sat at his desk and wondered, *What the hell is going on here?* He had an uneasy feeling that things were not going to end well for Pvt. Emily Stone. She was an angry young soldier.

Chapter Five

Emily awoke before 7:00 a.m., just as the sun started to peek into her room. Emily looked around the room.

"Where the hell am I?" said Emily out loud.

Then all came flooding back. She was on the run, she murdered Dr. Benson, and she was on her way to South Dakota to continue to enact her revenge. Emily jumped into the shower to fully wake up. After dressing, she took her toothbrush and headed to the car. The waitress told her there was an ATM at the Circle K, so Emily headed there to gas up the car and get some money. She also bought a couple doughnuts and a cup of coffee. The breakfast at the Super 8 didn't look appetizing and the coffee cups are too small. Emily then headed up to the Family Dollar. There she bought two pairs of jeans, clean underwear, T-shirts, a hoodie, and a pair of sneakers. She also picked up toothpaste along with other toiletries and a large travel bag. After she paid for everything, she walked back to the fitting room and changed into clean underwear, a pair of jeans, and one of the T-shirts. Outside the Family Dollar, she threw her old clothes in the trash. She sat in the car long enough to eat the doughnuts and hit the road again.

*****

At DTI online, students' personal information is not provided to other students; however, it's a common practice for online instructors to ask students to do introductions. Students are often open with information and comment about where they live. Emily knew that Colin Kennedy lived in Miller, South Dakota, from his introduction in a course, but she didn't know where in Miller. She also knew that he worked at the ACE Hardware in Miller. Colin mentioned he was in the cybersecurity program so he could have a better career than working at ACE Hardware. That was all that Emily knew about Colin but would need to find out more about him. She'd cross that bridge when she got closer, using her phone to find him.

A couple hours on the road, it was time to stop for a break, the coffee was going through her. Emily gassed up the car and hit the convenience store. She came out with a couple bottles of water and some snacks. Then it was back on the road.

While driving up I29, Emily thought, *I need a pistol. My KA-BAR may not work with Colin. I really have no idea how big of a guy he is.*

Her next stop up I29 would be Sioux Falls and to find a pawnshop. Going to Scheels wasn't going to work because of the three-day waiting period.

But…if I can find the right pawnshop, I might get someone to let me walk out with a pistol using my military ID. Maybe that would work with a sob story about heading out for a family emergency and not stopping at home before driving back to South Dakota. After all, it is South Dakota where everyone has a gun, thought Emily.

An hour after arriving in Sioux Falls, she left with a Glock, a box of ammunition, and a full tank of gas. Emily used her credit card for the purchase and gas. The way she figured it, when this is over, she would be on the run. She'd have to have a new identity. She might as well use this card to its max and not worry about it. She wasn't worried about her credit right about now.

Emily took the Brookings exit off I29 to Route 14. Brookings is the home of South Dakota State University, and from where Emily grew up near Ramona, this was the "big city." Her family would come to Brookings to do their shopping. Emily drove through Brookings then Volga, Arlington, and on toward Huron. She started to panic and pulled off the road.

"What am I going to do? How can I get to Colin? I need a plan!"

Chapter Six

Fall in the Upper Midwest means shades of yellow on the few trees you see on the plains. Then it gets damn cold. April McKenzie was driving along I29 to attend a meeting in Watertown. Part of April's responsibilities as director of DTI Online is to build relationships with other colleges for potential transfers to DTI. April was on her way to Lake Area Technical Institute for such a meeting. Statistics show that many online students live within driving distance of the college or university they attend. However, because most students are working adults, they cannot attend classes on campus. Online programs are their path to higher education. Lake Area Tech is a two-year institution. April's meeting there is to discuss transfer agreements from Lake Area's two-year programs to DTI's four-year programs using online delivery. It is not an easy pathway from a tech school to a traditional college, but April has been working with faculty from both institutions to find common ground in syllabi so that students are not forced to take courses needlessly.

On the three-hour drive to Watertown, April started thinking about fall in Central Pennsylvania. The maples turn beautiful shades of red, orange, and yellow, the oak trees with their deep vibrant maroon. The Pennsylvania mountainsides would be a patchwork of color. April's mind was starting to wonder back to her youth and her grandmother. Fall was a time for baking. April loved her grandma's pies, especially shoofly pie. Shoofly pie is a popular Amish dessert. It is a molasses crumb pie, but the Amish call it "shoo fly" because the Amish women would put the pies on windowsills to cool which would draw flies, which they would "shoo" away, thus the nickname shoofly pie. It was one of April's favorite and her grandmother taught her how to bake it. Her grandmother made a wet-bottom pie, which is so gooey and yummy. When you find shoofly pie for sale outside the Amish community, you will get a dry shoofly pie, mostly crumbs and little molasses.

April thought to herself, *I ought to bake one, it's been a while.*

She continued thinking of home and the holidays. Christmas brought to mind both of her grandmothers' special sweets like pinwheels and divinity.

Damn, thought April. *I should have eaten lunch before I left.*

April hadn't been herself since she heard about Gloria Benson. She had called Gloria's husband to express her condolences and had sent flowers on behalf of DTI Online, but she couldn't attend the funeral and April felt badly about that. There hadn't been any follow-up contact with Det. Smiley since she had sent the file on the online cheating group. She didn't know if there was any progress on finding Gloria's killer. Of course, it had only been a few hours.

As she sped up I-29, little did April know she was driving the same highway as the killer.

Chapter Seven

Emily pulled off the side of road at a rest stop and checked to see if she had cell signal. Out on the plains of South Dakota, cell service is spotty at best. However, service was getting better and she found she had four bars.

Good, she thought.

Emily pulled out a granola bar she picked up, opened her last bottle of water, and started searching Miller, South Dakota. Miller is the county seat for Hand County with a population just over 1400. Miller had a nicely set up business directory on its website. Emily had no problem finding the address for the Miller ACE Hardware and she saw there was also a Super 8.

Emily began formulating her plan. "First, I'll go check into the Super 8, then I'll go investigate the Ace Hardware. I'll need to find out which employee is Colin and when the store closes, I'll follow him home. Once I see where Colin lives and works, I can plan his demise from there."

Having boosted her body and her mind, Emily got back on the road.

As she cruised into Miller, Emily found the Super 8 easy enough. She checked into her room and again, she found the room to be clean but dated like the one she stayed at the night before. Emily laid down on the bed for a few minutes to clear her mind. It's a small town and it shouldn't be hard to follow Colin home but that doesn't mean he lives in town. So Emily decided to get the car gassed up before she went to the hardware. After freshening up, Emily headed out, gassed up the car, and found the hardware. It was going on five o'clock, she was hoping the store was still open. It was and she walked inside, looking around quickly then headed up an aisle. She wasn't paying attention to what was in the aisle, she was looking for the employees.

A voice behind her asked, "Can I help you with something?"

Emily turned around and found herself looking directly at Colin Kennedy. She knew it was Colin by his name tag. Emily's heart skipped a beat. He was tall and lanky; wearing jeans, a flannel shirt, and cowboy boots, Colin was extremely handsome with dirty-blond hair and bright-blue eyes.

Emily stammered a second and said, "I'm looking for some rope."

Colin replied, "Sorry, didn't mean to startle you. It's in the next aisle."

Emily was relieved that it wasn't in the aisle she was in. Colin walked her to the next aisle and showed her the rope. Emily thanked him and muttered something about going to just look around some and thanked him again.

Oh my god, thought Emily. *I didn't expect to walk right into him.* She was flustered and needed to get a grip on herself. Emily picked up fifty feet of rope, some garbage bags, and duct tape. *I'm not sure what I am going to do yet*, thought Emily, *but these might come in handy.*

She paid the young girl at the checkout and walked out, looking at the store hours on the door as she left.

The store closes at five thirty; I'll drive around back to see if employees park back there, thought Emily.

Emily spotted a Bronco and an old pickup. Emily pulled around front and parked down the street, about half a block, in a spot where she could see if he came out front at five thirty or she could see him if he comes around front in the Bronco or pickup.

About five thirty-five, Emily spotted the old pickup coming around from the back and turning right. She saw it was Colin, so she started her car and pulled out, following about a block behind him. He headed west out of Miller on Route 14. He went about five miles and turned onto a paved county road heading south. It was getting dark quickly as it does in early fall. Emily was hoping he'd turn off soon or she would have to turn her headlights on and then he'd know there was a car behind him. Just as she was about to turn her headlights on, Colin turned left on to a gravel driveway. Emily drove on past, turning on her headlights and a quarter mile down the road made a U-turn, slowly coming back past the driveway. Squinting to read the mailbox as she passed, she saw the name Kennedy.

Well, that wasn't too hard, thought Emily but then she realized she was going to have to do reconnaissance up that driveway to the house. That wasn't going to be easy; she had no idea what was up there and how she would get up there without being seen.

But that's for later, thought Emily.

She was hungry, so she drove back to town to get something at the Dairy Queen she saw on the way out of town. She could go for a burger, fries, and a Blizzard.

Emily grabbed her dinner from the drive-through and headed back to her room. She chowed down on her burger and fries. As she settled back to enjoy her Reese's Peanut Butter Cup Blizzard, she turned on the TV to check out the local news.

"It will be a good idea to see if anything is going on in the state."

Not only will Emily need to plan what's in store for Colin, but she will need to plan for her escape. The news talked about the buffalo round up in Custer and a bunch of local fall festivals.

Nothing too much to worry about, thought Emily. *I can easily leave the state when I am done, just need to figure out where to go.*

Emily's mind started to wander. *Who is Colin Kennedy? I know he is married with kids; but I don't know how old they are or if his wife works. What's up the gravel road?* A little panic set in. *What the hell are you doing, Emily Stone? You ruined your career by cheating, you've ruined your life by killing your instructor, and now you are planning to kill again.*

Emily has rationalized this all along by blaming everyone else but herself and she quickly went back to that mindset. Why did Mr. High-and-Mighty Colin Kennedy find it that damn important to turn her in for cheating? It wasn't hurting him any. He was like top in the class. So while Emily was still hot, she started to plan how to do her reconnaissance of his home.

Since this was a farming community, the Ace Hardware opened early. Which meant that Colin would probably head in early. Emily just didn't know if Colin's wife worked, at what time, and if any of the kids would catch the bus, and so on. She would have to go out early and sit a short way down and across the road from his driveway to watch for everyone leaving. Once the coast was clear, she could cross over and sneak up the shelter belt. Most all farms and properties in the South Dakotan countryside have a shelter belt of trees to block the wind that constantly blows across the plains and to protect from blowing snow. Emily just hoped there were no big dogs. She was not much of a dog person and farm dogs often aren't overly friendly to strangers.

After formulating her plan over in her head a few times to make sure she had it down pat, Emily took a long shower and fell asleep watching TV. She woke once to the static of the TV, set her alarm to be ready by 6:00 a.m. to grab coffee and something from the continental breakfast on her way down the road.

Tuesday

Chapter Eight

Emily rolled out of bed a little slowly in the early, dark morning. The travel and the stress were getting to her, she just wanted to roll over and sleep some more but knew she couldn't. Clearly, her training to rise and shine and exercise first thing in the morning was quickly wearing off. After dressing and brushing her teeth, Emily headed out to the continental breakfast. She grabbed a couple muffins and two cups of coffee.

Why do they use such small cups? thought Emily. *Cheapskates!*

It wasn't quite daylight when Emily pulled off the road a few hundred yards down from the Kennedy driveway. She settled in to eat her muffins, which were as dry as the Sahara Desert. She washed them down with the coffee, which wasn't too bad but not enough of it.

"Boy, I wish I had brought a couple bottles of water."

As she finished up, Emily checked out the landscape. Wide ditches are common on all South Dakota roads. Ditches are used for snowmobiles in the winter. There are small traffic signs in the ditches just for snowmobile traffic. It wasn't snowmobile season yet, but Emily again thought back about her childhood in Ramona and wished she was back to those simpler times.

Maybe life on the farm wasn't as bad as I thought. We'd ride snow-mobiles on a Sunday afternoon and come back to hot chocolate and whatever cookies Mom had baked... Emily shook her head and said to herself, "Snap out of it. You need to be looking at the landscape toward Colin's driveway and house."

There was a wire fence at the edge of the ditch and the shelter-belt starting about thirty yards up the drive. Dotted along the way were a few bushes including some lilacs. Lilacs grow well in South

Dakota and are often grown as snow shelter. This property has a scraggly looking shelterbelt.

Looking at the state of the shelterbelt, it must be an older farm and farmhouse, she thought.

Just then, Emily spotted the old pickup coming down the gravel road and turning toward Route 14. It was Colin and he was by himself. She quickly slid down on the seat so Colin wouldn't see her; she wasn't able to see that Colin took a quick look her car as he drove by. Seeing an abandoned car along the road was unusual. Emily sat up and not long after Colin headed into town, Emily could see a school bus come down the road. At the same time, an older Camry came down the driveway. The school bus came to a stop and a small boy jumped out of the car and climbed into the bus.

"Well, that answers one thing, one of his kids goes to school."

Colin's wife didn't turn right toward Route 14 but turned left. Not sure where she is going, Emily thought she should sit tight a little longer.

It was a good thing that Emily stayed in the car observing the landscape. Ten minutes later, the Camry came back up the road. It didn't turn back in the driveway but continued on toward Route 14. Emily wondered why the short trip down the road.

"Ah, maybe she was taking the other child to daycare."

Emily decided to follow the Camry and see where his wife is going; does she work? So Emily started her car and fell in behind the Camry. It's so flat she could hang back as not to raise suspicion. As the Camry reached Route 14, it turned east toward Miller.

Emily started to move in closer to the Camry as they began to reach Miller. Emily saw Colin's wife pull around behind the Curl Up and Dye Beauty Shop, so she pulled in a parking spot across the street.

Is she getting her hair done or does she work there? wondered Emily.

She soon had her answer, she saw Colin's wife walk in front of the window with one of those black hairdresser's frocks on.

So she works there. Good, thought Emily. *I can go back to the house and do some reconnaissance.*

Emily went to Casey's for some drinks and snacks and headed back to Colin's place. She wanted to get the layout of the place so she can decide how she was going to do him in. She parked across the road, a little way from the drive, crossed the highway, walked through the field and up the back side of the shelter belt. Living out in the country, most people have dogs and sometimes farm animals. Emily wondered if Colin did. It didn't take long for a black lab to wonder over her way. He was friendly and walked with her as she approached an outbuilding. She saw a modest ranch house with two car garage and a shed.

"It's a nice place," muttered Emily.

However, there is not much in the way of shelter for a surprise attack on Colin without his wife seeing. So she patted the lab good-bye and worked her way through the shelter belt and back to her vehicle. She sat in her car, snacking and working on her plan.

Emily knew that she needed to do this and get out of here soon. She thought about parking her car right near Colin's driveway early the next morning, putting the hood up like she was having car trouble. Knowing Colin from class discussions and from turning her group in for cheating, she figured he would stop to see if he could help.

"He was a goody two shoes!"

Emily knew she would have to time it right so that no one else on the road would stop. It will be tricky, but it might work.

It will mean I use the KA-BAR instead of the Glock, thought Emily. *A shot may attract attention.*

Feeling satisfied with her plan, she thought it might be a good night to go out and have a couple beers. Emily would stop in the Turtle Creek Saloon tonight to have a burger and a couple beers, maybe chat up some of the locals, saying she had stopped for the night on her way west river to visit a friend, taking the scenic route instead of I90. She'll have to let the front desk at the Super 8 know she'll be checking out in the morning. She headed back to her room to get organized and have her to-go bag for leaving in the morning. She did a quick load of clothes at the coin-operated washer and dryer in the motel. There was a change machine by the washer. She put a five-dollar bill in it and took every bit of it until she paid for some detergent and dryer sheet out of the machine and pay for the washer and dryer.

Geesh, thought Emily. *What a rip-off.*

After Emily had her go bag ready, she stopped to get some cash from the ATM to tide her over for a while on her way to the bar.

"Paying all these ATM charges is adding up. This is getting to be an expensive venture," grumbled Emily.

Emily actually enjoyed her evening at the Turtle Creek Saloon. The bar was like so many in the small towns of South Dakota. Some of them might have some older booths but many just had folding tables and chairs. Even though the atmosphere may not be the greatest, the food was always good and the comradery was outstanding. The small bars in small towns were the town's social center.

When Emily walked into the Turtle Creek, she looked around for where to sit. There were a couple families at the tables having dinner, so Emily decided to sit at the bar. There was a couple at the bar, at least she assumed they were. Emily sat a seat down from the woman. The bartender brought her the menu and asked her what she wanted to drink. Emily ordered a beer and asked how the burgers were. The bartender said they were the best in the area. So Emily ordered the bacon cheeseburger and fries.

The bartender asked Emily if she was from around here.

Emily let her guard down a little and responded, "I'm from the Ramona area originally. I am back doing some visiting and am headed out west river to see some friends. I thought I'd take the scenic route on 34 rather than drive out I90." That seemed to break the ice.

Hank was the bartender and he asked her name.

Emily responded, "Emily." She didn't think it would hurt. She would be gone in the morning.

Hank asked, "What made you leave Ramona?"

Emily responded, "I wanted to get out of small town, farm country. I joined the army to see the world."

So Hank asked if she did see the world.

Emily laughed. "Never got out of the US. I wanted to go into cybersecurity and that is located at Fort Gordon in Georgia. At least, I got away from the cold winters."

Hank laughed and then brought Emily her burger.

As Emily was finishing her meal, Hank brought her a beer.

The look that Emily gave Hank made him smile and he said, "It's from Carla and Mike." As he nodded to the couple beside her.

Carla turned to Emily and said, "Welcome to Miller."

Emily, Carla, Mike, and Hank sat and chatted over a few beers for the better part of two hours.

Indeed, the bar was nice, the food at the Turtle Creek Salon was great, and Emily enjoyed talking to the locals in the bar. She had been on such a mission to exact revenge for being wronged that she had lost touch with people. After she left and went back to the Super 8, she settled up her bill at the front desk on her way to her room. She told them she would be out early on her way to west river.

Emily lay on her bed and wondered what she was doing. She thought about being suspended from her online cybersecurity program. It was so important to her, for advancement in her military career. But that was over now. She was AWOL and wondered how and when the army would start looking for her. Once again, she started to get furious. There was one more person she had to deal with. And that was Reggie Smith. After she offed Colin, she needed to head to Bolton and hook up with Haley Jorgeson to exact her revenge on the program staff person responsible for her suspension. Her resolve and the few beers put Emily right to sleep.

Chapter Nine

April was sitting at her desk going through her morning email, a tedious job at best, when Lori buzzed her.

"Det. Smiley is on the phone for you," announced Lori.

"Put him through," said April.

"Good morning, Dr. McKenzie," started Det. Smiley. "I was wondering if you had time to talk about Dr. Benson's murder?"

"Sure," April replied.

Det. Smiley continued. "I have been reviewing the information you sent me, and I was wondering if this murderer could possibly be the disgruntled military student, Pvt. Stone? The coroner has suggested that the murderer used a knife similar to a KA-BAR. Your military student with her complaints against Dr. Benson would have possession of that particular knife, it's standard army issue. This murder is very personal in nature and so far, we have not come up with anyone else in Dr. Benson's life here who would have had a strong motive to hurt Dr. Benson. I see that there were multiple student complaints about Dr. Benson, so now I am looking at her students."

April took a second to gather herself before responding. She deals with a lot of student problems but never thought about a student actually doing an instructor harm.

She responded, "Det. Smiley, I have worked with online students for years and although I have had some seriously upset students, I wouldn't think any of them would kill over it, even Pvt. Emily Stone. Dr. Benson was a tough instructor but fair. She does receive her fair share of complaints. Gloria was a biology instructor and teaching any science online is not easy. She expected a certain level of work from her students and if they didn't meet it, they were graded accordingly."

April continued. "One thing that bothers me is how a student knew where Dr. Benson lived. The students are not provided personal information on their instructors, such as home phone numbers and where they live. We encourage our instructors to provide only email address and phone numbers, only if they will except calls. However, providing phone numbers is not encouraged, for such situations such as the harassment Pvt. Stone was doing to Dr. Benson." April thought for a second and added, "However, most of these students are in technology programs, such as our cybersecurity program. They would have the skill set needed to find out where someone lives."

"I thought that might be the case," said Smiley. "That is why I called. You had mentioned Pvt. Stone and after reviewing your files, I'm beginning to think she is a strong suspect."

April responded that DTI Online has many military students in their online technology degrees. "They are really interested in our technology programs and really love to take the technology and computer-based courses. These students find the general education courses are of no interest and that is where I get the complaints. The general education courses are required and where we find the most cheating going on. Those who do refer to cheating think it is the way to get through the general education courses. Pvt. Stone was one such student."

Smiley commented he noticed that and remembered Dr. Benson was one of instructors involved in the big cheating ring discovered by DTI Online.

Oh that, thought April. "Yes," said April. "There were military students in that incident and a staff member from here. One of the most vocal students out of that mess was Emily Stone. In fact, when she was suspended from the cybersecurity program, she starting to make some of those threatening comments to Dr. Benson. We reported it to her superiors. She also received a reprimand there too. Her harassment of Dr. Benson kept heating up. I believe Dr. Benson's husband had gone to the police. He was going out of town and wanted to have some police drive by occasionally as he was gone."

"Dang," replied Smiley. "That reminds me, I need to follow up with Pvt. Stone's commanding officer."

Once Det. Smiley ended the call with April, he set about finding the contact information for Emily's unit at Fort Gordon. After some bureaucratic runaround with the Fort switchboard, Smiley finally reached the lieutenant in Emily Stone's unit. Smiley identified himself and inquired about the whereabouts of Pvt. Stone. The young lieutenant briefly stated that Pvt. Stone had not reported for duty yesterday and that Det. Smiley would need to speak to the Fort commander. Det. Smiley was then forwarded to LTG Cook, Fort Gordon's Commander.

Smiley started out. "Good afternoon, LTG Cook, I am Det. Darius Smiley from the Birmingham Police Department. I am calling to inquire about the whereabouts of Pvt. Emily Stone. She is a person of interest in a murder investigation here in Birmingham."

Taken back a little, Cook responded, "Currently, Pvt. Emily Stone is considered AWOL. I am surprised to hear that Pvt. Stone is a person of interest in a murder, but I was going to reach out to the director of DTI Online about the cheating situation that Pvt. Stone was involved in, and to whether it would have any bearing on Pvt. Stone currently being AWOL."

Smiley responded, "I can fill you in on that investigation. I have spoken to Dr. April McKenzie several times and we discussed the cheating incident Pvt. Stone was involved in. When she was caught within a cheating ring that was discovered by DTI Online staff, it was Pvt. Stone's biology instructor, Dr. Gloria Benson, who had reported Pvt. Stone, among others, to Dr. McKenzie and her staff. It appears it was quite a large operation which included an employee of the program, Pvt. Stone, and other students. The employee was fired and Stone along with other students were suspended from their programs. Since then, Pvt. Stone has made increasingly threatening messages to Dr. Benson to the point where her husband called the department concerned about her safety. He was going to be out of town this past weekend. After we reviewed the numerous emails, we decided to do drive by surveillance of the home while Mr. Benson was out of town. Sadly, the surveillance was not sufficient. Mr. Benson came home to find his wife murdered. After speaking to Dr. McKenzie, I discovered that, at that time, she had informed Stone's supervisor here at the

Fort about the situation and she was under the understanding that disciplinary actions had been taken against Pvt. Stone. I wanted to touch base with you on this matter."

LTG Cook replied, "Yes, the incident was reported to her supervisor. When Pvt. Stone was reported AWOL yesterday, I had an uneasy feeling about it. Not only was Pvt. Stone suspended from her academic program at DTI Online, she received a formal reprimand here. This situation has basically stopped her career advancement, but she has been walking the line with her work in her unit. As part of the AWOL process, I have the authority to declare a special category absentee because of her work in cybersecurity. She isn't a huge security risk, but I am concerned. The special category absentee status allows for contact with the family without waiting the required ten days. I spoke with Pvt. Stone's mother yesterday. She commented that Pvt. Stone is in contact with her family only every month or so. However, she also told me on her last call with Emily, she was very upset with her biology instructor. I believe the issues with this instructor are very serious."

With this start of a conversation, Det. Smiley and LTG Cook made a plan on keeping each other informed of any information they might find. Det. Smiley told LTG Cook he would keep Dr. McKenzie on the loop; however, he did provide her contact information to Cook in case he needed it.

Wednesday

Chapter Ten

Emily was up and gone by 6:00 a.m.; no coffee or breakfast this morning. She was too keyed up to eat. Emily hurried out of Miller and headed to the Kennedy's. She had positioned her car off the road only a few feet from Colin's drive. There was not very much traffic on the road, but she kept herself scrunched down in the seat, so the car looked empty. Emily was glad there was little traffic and when it was about time for Colin to come down the drive, she slid out of her car and lifted up the hood.

Emily had her KA-BAR in her jacket pocket. Colin was taller than her, so she needed the element of surprise. It will not be as easy as killing Dr. Benson.

Emily heard his truck coming down the driveway. She got out of her car and stood at the hood of her car, looking at the engine with a flashlight.

As expected, Colin pulled in behind her and got out of his truck.

"Do you need some help?" asked Colin.

Emily responded, "Yes, my car made a funny noise and just stopped as I pulled over. I have no idea what's wrong with it."

Colin responded, "Let me take a look. You know, I saw a car similar to this yesterday morning."

That threw Emily off for a few seconds. She should have known he'd be that observant. But Emily was determined.

As Colin was bent over the engine to look, just as he was saying "I don't see anything—"

Emily pulled the knife from her pocket and stepped up beside him. She put the knife up against his side and said, "My name is Emily Stone and you cost me my future."

As Colin turned to look at her, she sliced his leg and as he fell, she slit his throat. Colin gasped for air with fear in his eyes. He lay in front of her car, bleeding out.

Emily looked down at herself. There was so much blood on her hands, her jacket, and jeans. She didn't realize there would be so much blood. There was a car coming in the distance. She needed to pull herself together and get the hell out of here. Emily slammed the hood of the car shut, started it up, backed up, and did a U-turn, then headed south. Panic set in.

Chapter Eleven

As Julie came down the driveway, she saw Colin's truck.

"Why is Colin's truck sitting off the road? Where is Colin?"

Soon she had her answer, she saw Colin laying along the road. Julie pulled off the road. She told Dylan and Susan to stay in the car and she ran to Colin. Julie saw the blood and stopped dead.

"Don't panic, don't panic. Remember, the kids are in the car."

She pulled her phone out of her pocket and called 911. Julie knew in her heart Colin was dead. She also knew that it would take time for the ambulance to get there. Julie waived the school bus on by and walked back to her car and got in the car.

Dylan asked his mom, "What's wrong with Daddy?"

Julie responded, "Daddy's sick. Mommy has called for the ambulance and I wanted to make sure you guys are okay. We will sit here till the ambulance comes." Julie thought about it for a few minutes and decided to call her sitter, Angie. "Could Jim, Angie's husband, come up to the house and pick up the kids? There's an accident by the house."

Angie said "sure" and asked if everything was okay.

Julie replied that Jim will fill her in, but that she might need to keep the kids for a while.

It seemed like forever, but Jim and the ambulance arrived about the same time. Julie told Dylan and Susan that Jim was going to take them to the sitter while Mommy took care of Daddy. Jim had pulled past Julie's car and got out and so did Julie. He had seen Colin laying there. Julie was trying not to break down and cry in front of the kids.

"Jim, I don't know what happened but I know he's dead. I told the kids that he is sick. I'm not sure what happened or when I can come for the kids."

Jim said not to worry, and he hurried Dylan and Susan to his truck. "Call us when you can, we are praying for you." And Jim drove off with her children.

As the ambulance crew was unloading, Deputy Shane Anderson pulled in. With her children gone, Julie broke down. Deputy Anderson went over to the ambulance crew who quickly told him that the man was deceased and it was clear he had been murdered. They would call the coroner. Then Deputy Anderson walked up to Julie.

"Ma'am, I need your help, can you talk to me?"

Julie knew she had to pull herself together. She took a deep breath. "He is my husband. I came down the drive with the kids and I saw him lying there. When I walked toward him, I knew he was dead. I called 911 and sat with my kids. I didn't want them to know what was going on. I told them Daddy is sick. I called for the sitter to pick them up, they live just down the road. When they were gone, I just lost it." And Julie started sobbing again.

Deputy Anderson was taking a long look at the wife as she talked with him. She was a beautiful woman with long dark hair and bright-blue eyes. She was full of poise, even in this situation, crying and brokenhearted.

In a soft voice, Deputy Anderson said, "I know this is hard, but I need to know your name and your husband's name."

Julie took another breath. "I'm Julie Kennedy, and that is my husband, Colin."

Again, in soft voice, Deputy Anderson, "Mrs. Kennedy, it appears that your husband has been murdered." At that time the ambulance crew walked up to Julie and the Deputy. "Please help her to calm down some. I do need to get more information from her, so please try not to sedate her," commented Deputy Anderson.

Deputy Anderson then called headquarters. "I need the state police CSI team here. I have a murder."

There are not many murders in the area so it will be big news. Deputy Anderson noticed that the victim had his throat slit. Not a pleasant way to go but quick. What could have happened in his life to have caused this? Anderson knew he needed more information from his wife, so he walked over to the ambulance. Julie seemed a little calmer. Just as Deputy Anderson got to the ambulance, Julie's phone rang. Deputy Anderson listened to her end of the conversation.

"Oh, I'm so sorry, I won't be in today… Something has happened. Please cancel my appointments… Yes, cancel them… As I came down the drive, I saw Colin's truck and I saw him lying on the road… More than hurt, he's dead… I have to go now; the police wants to talk to me."

Deputy Anderson asked Julie if she was able to talk. Julie nodded. Anderson asked her to walk through what happened.

Julie started, "I work at a beauty salon in Miller and I was coming down the drive to put Dylan on the school bus and take Susan to the sitter. They live five miles down the road. I saw Colin's truck and saw him lying there."

Deputy Anderson gave her a second and asked her, "So your husband leaves for work before you?"

"Yes," Julie said.

"So it appears that Colin never made it into work. You hadn't heard from Colin's employer?" asked Deputy Anderson.

"No," responded Julie. "But I bet there are messages on his cell and probably now on our home phone."

Deputy Anderson received an incoming call. When he was done, he told the ambulance crew and Julie that the state CSI team should be here within forty-five minutes and the coroner within an hour. He asked the crew to place a blanket or sheet over Colin, being careful not to disturb anything. He didn't want passersby to witness the body. The news would get out fast enough. And then told the ambulance crew that they could leave. He would stay with Mrs. Kennedy until the CSI team and the coroner arrives. The ambulance crew asked if Julie needed anything else, left her with a bottle of water, and then left after giving Julie their condolences.

Deputy Anderson then said to Julie, "I know this is hard, just leaving Colin like this, but we need to leave the crime scene alone until the crime scene team arrives. Then we can go up to your house while they continue the investigation. We cannot move Colin until the CSI team has completed their investigation. The coroner will take Colin and conduct an autopsy to determine cause of death, but I have to tell you it appears his throat was cut and he bled out quickly. It was quick. Do you have any idea who might have done this to him?"

Julie Kennedy sobbed again and just shook her head no. Deputy Anderson could see that shock was starting to set in. He asked Julie if there was anybody she'd like him to call. Julie replied that her parents live outside of Huron. Colin's parents live west river and Julie wanted to call them when she was all done here. She wanted to have all the information she could when she called. He took down their information and gave them a call. By then, the CSI team had arrived along with another deputy to watch out for passing traffic. Deputy Anderson told Julie that her parents were on their way and asked if she was ready to move on up to the house.

The rest of the morning and into the afternoon, the CSI team worked diligently to process the scene. The coroner showed up at the scene and placed Colin's body in a body bag with the help of the CSI team and loaded it up in his van to take to the morgue. News traveled fast and by the time Julie's parents had arrived, Julie's phone was ringing nonstop. Julie talked it over with Deputy Anderson and she asked to call Colin's family to tell them what happened, which she did.

Although Julie was totally drained by the time Colin's body had been moved, she wanted her children at home. She needed to explain to them, as best she could, what happened to their father. She asked her father to go to Jim and Angie's to pick up the kids. Julie's mother busied herself in the kitchen, where Julie could hear her sobbing. Julie's head was just spinning. "WHY DID THIS HAPPEN?"

Deputy Anderson returned to the sheriff's office to write up his report.

This case is going to be hard to solve, thought Shane. *We have no clue as to why this happened. But there is a dangerous killer out there.*

Chapter Twelve

Pvt. Emily Stone was speeding down the highway having just murdered a second person. Her life was unraveling before her. She had to get a grip, she had to get rid of her bloody clothes and the KA-BAR, and she had to get to Haley Jorgenson.

Haley Jorgenson worked in student services at DTI Online. She was also working on her degree in business information systems at DTI. Or at least she had been.

Haley was a high school graduate, just barely. School just didn't interest her. She applied to DTI for a job, as most in the area did. She had good people skills and she liked working with students, so she eventually wound up in DTI Online as a student support specialist. Students working on online programs were a little different from campus students. They were older, they had jobs and kids, and many were in the military. They had way more interesting lives than traditional students and had unique issues for Haley to help with. Haley really enjoyed her job and she saw there was a chance to advance in DTI Online, so she decided she should get her degree.

Haley soon found that she related to many of her students when it came to taking her general education courses. She should have paid more attention in high school. Haley loved working with technology, but English, math, biology, and history were not her thing. Haley started looking at the open forums that some instructors set up in the online courses. It was a way for students to connect with each other and for students who were doing well in the course to help mentor those who needed it. Haley noticed that she had many of the same students in her courses, some of them in the same program. She reached out to a few students to see if they wanted to connect outside of the courses. The students were ones she worked with in student services. She had access to their personal information and she knew they lived in the area.

What turned out to be a study group ended up being a cheating ring. The group of five started meeting once a week to study. One evening, when studying at Haley's for an online test, Haley suggested that she log in to the exam and they follow through the exam with her and record questions and possible answers and try to figure them out while she was taking the exam.

At DTI Online, the students used a learning management system where the students would log into and access the course they were taking. Within that system, students would find their lessons, homework, quizzes, exams, projects, etc. When taking an exam or quiz, there was a remote proctoring system where a 360-degree camera was provided to students and then they sat in front of the camera to take their exams. Being recorded while taking the exams and then having the recording saved on a server allows for the instructors to check to see if anyone was cheating. Exams are timed and the questions are delivered in random order. There are many ways to prevent cheating, but it seems that some students would rather try to skirt the system and cheat rather than learn course material.

That is what Haley's group of five were doing. The others stayed out of sight and split up who wrote down the question and wrote down the potential answers. Haley completed the exam and submitted it. Sometimes, the scores would come up right away, depending on how the instructor set up the exam. The group would figure out the answers and each would login from Haley's computer and take their exam. Members of the group each took turns to be the one who took the exam first, as that score was never the best. But they soon had a pattern down on how to pass the quizzes and exams. However, the group started to get sloppy and members of the group could be seen on camera during their exams.

Their system was working well. Until one day, when Haley was talking to one of her students, Pvt. Emily Stone. Emily was complaining about how hard it was to get through some of the general education courses. Haley had a moment of weakness and mentioned what her group was doing. However, Haley said she would consider helping her out with text and quiz information for a price. Emily was more than willing to pay and so Haley started a sideline. The group of five still worked through the required general education courses and unbeknownst to them, Haley had a sideline of recommending courses and providing course information for a fee. Haley covered her program costs with her side business. Haley just had a knack to know which students would be interested in her offer.

However, all good things or bad things must come to an end. The head of the DTI Online Technology Services decided that his staff needed to start spot checking course exam videos for cheating, as many instructors opted not to. Cheating in online courses has always been a concern. Although it is only a small group of all online students, their actions have tainted the image of online students.

Reggie Smith was the technology troubleshooter who was assigned the task of reviewing exam video, which is done twice a year. It was a tedious job, so he decided to enlist Levi to assist. Levi is a student in the cybersecurity program, who works part-time at Best Buy in Sioux City, Iowa, and currently interns in the IT department of DTI Online. The staff reviews of the exam videos would find the occasional student who was using the textbook or notes when not approved by the instructor. But some video reviews were also very comical; Reggie was surprised at what people would wear and do while in front of the camera. In a speech course, one student was recording her speech while driving on I85 in Atlanta, another student recorded her speech in her bathrobe, which kept coming open. All students knew that they were being recorded and the video was subject to review. Reggie and Levi would note all the students' names and courses, where it happened, and anything else that was out of the ordinary.

This time, Levi was reviewing Dr. Benson's biology course. Dr. Benson had contacted Dr. McKenzie about her suspicions of cheating in her biology course. Math and science courses were often where Reggie and Levi found cheating. Levi brought a science exam to Reggie's attention. Levi recognized Haley from the office and it was clear that this was working in a group effort and they were cheating on the exam. Reggie decided to look up Haley's student record to see what other courses she was in. Reviewing some of the other courses Haley was in, Reggie discovered the group of five with Haley Jorgenson at the helm in the biology course. They had become complacent and worked clearly within view of the camera. Reggie went directly to the director of technology services, Bob Lundgren. Bob reviewed the video and looked at student rosters, checking IP addresses to confirm the student identities, then went straight to April. April called in Bev Peterson, the director of student services. When Dr. Benson had made a call to Dr. McKenzie about concerns in her course, she had mentioned Colin Kennedy had brought concerns about cheating to Dr. Benson. This was serious and after a few meetings to plan how to deal with the situation, Bev called Haley into April's office for a meeting.

Haley was in shock that her group had been found out. She was beside herself. Dr. McKenzie was firing her and threatening legal action against her and the others. Haley was in a real panic, the directors didn't know the half of it. If she was fired, when her replacement took over her student load, that person will surely find out about her side business with other students. Haley asked that if she came clean about everything, would they promise not to take legal action against her. Believing that this was a small group, the leadership team agreed. When it was all said and done, Haley was fired and thirty-seven students were suspended from their programs, including Pvt. Emily Stone who was in Dr. Benson's biology course at the time and had cheated on the exam. However, Emily wasn't angry with Haley for the whole scheme falling apart; they had become friends. But now Haley owed her big-time. She had taken care of Dr Benson and Colin, but now Emily would need Haley's help to eliminate Reggie Smith.

Chapter Thirteen

Emily thought to herself, *Slow down. You don't want to get pulled over. But you do need to find a place to get cleaned up and dump these clothes.*

Now that Emily had slowed down and was paying attention, she spied a rest area up ahead. In South Dakota, you would find the big rest areas with conveniences along the interstates. However, on the state roads, you will find pull offs; sometimes when you were lucky, there would be pit toilets. This rest area had some.

Perfect, and there is a small stream running nearby, thought Emily as she pulled off.

No one was there and she hadn't seen a car coming in either direction. Emily yanked off her jacket and left it in the back seat. She went over to the stream and washed the blood off her hands and face. Back at her car, Emily took out another pair of jeans and a sweatshirt.

Damn, she thought. *I will need to buy more clothes.*

Emily went into the outhouse and changed clothes. She stuffed the jeans, shirt, jacket, and KA-BAR into the hole of the outhouse. The smell of the pit toilet reminded Emily of her childhood. Nothing smells as bad as pit toilets and cow shit. Emily thought back to her childhood. Living on a farm, there was not a lot of vacation time but her dad had bought a second-hand camper and they would go to the state fair in Huron every summer. That was so much fun. Sometimes they would go to Lake Herman State Park outside Madison, especially around Prairie Days. She and her friends would often go to Lake Herman State Park just to hang out and swim. Those were good days.

Emily sat in her car and started to cry. "This is not what I wanted for my life, but I am in too deep and I will finish it. Reggie Smith is responsible for taking Haley down and because of Reggie and Colin, I was kicked out of my program. He's the last to go."

Emily was trying to figure exactly where she was. She looked across the road and saw a sign saying Yankton was 105 miles away. She knew then she was not quite two hours from Haley. She also realized how thirsty and hungry she was. She didn't take anything from the motel with her this morning. First place she saw to stop for something to eat, she'd do that.

Half an hour later, Emily came to a crossroads with gas and a convenience store. These convenience stores often had a little diner or something like a Subway. This place had Mean Gene's Pizza.

This will have to do, thought Emily.

Emily pulled into the parking lot, got out of her car, and stretched. Every part of her body hurt. This situation has her so stressed that every muscle hurt. "I haven't hurt this bad since basic training."

Emily settled for an individual pepperoni pizza and two bottles of water. She sat at one of the tables that were set up by the front window. While Emily sat eating her dried out, overheated pizza, she was startled by the sound of sirens coming her way. Panic set in. But the sheriff's car rolled through the intersection past the convenience store.

"This is no way to live," Emily said to herself. "I need to take care of this and move on. Maybe to Arizona. I can get lost there; nobody will know me."

Before she left, she looked for a heavy sweatshirt or jacket since she had to dump her jacket. She also had to see if they carried cell phones. Her parents had been calling but she wasn't picking up. She knew the army would have contacted her parents. Although she would like her mother to know she was okay, she couldn't let her know. They would call the army. It was time to dump this phone so she couldn't be tracked. Emily hadn't been thinking about covering her tracks but at least she could dump this phone so no one could track it. Emily purchased a cell phone and a one-month activation plan. She activated the new phone while sitting in her car, transferring her contacts, deleting everything on the old phone, and she threw the old phone in the trash.

Chapter Fourteen

April sat in her office, not able to concentrate on work. Overnight, April had been thinking about the possibility of a student killing an instructor. She could not imagine that a student would hurt an instructor. April always looked for the best in people when she was dealing with her students and her faculty. However, she also had to realize that the program did serve all kinds of students, including a number of military students who have all kinds of special defensive training. She had to agree that indeed a student could have killed Dr. Benson. It made her sick to think about it, especially that this could be one of the military students, Emily Stone. Although some of the military students are the best students in the programs, she had to face that it could be true. April wanted to talk to Det. Smiley about it again. She wondered if it would be helpful to email instructors about any incidents that they dealt with which had not involved her or anyone else in the office. Many instructors handle classroom situations without ever mentioning them to the office.

April reached for the phone and called Det. Smiley.

When she got through to Det. Smiley, his first comment was, "I was just going to call you." Smiley went on to say that he had contacted Pvt. Stone's commanding officer. "It appears that Emily Stone has gone AWOL. She has been missing since the day after Dr. Benson's murder."

April was in shock. Could this really be happening? She told Det. Smiley she was having a hard time believing this is happening. He understood. They talked a couple minutes about what had happened.

Then Det. Smiley said, "You called me, how can I help you?"

April explained her ideas about how many instructors do handle classroom situations without ever involving the office. She wondered if it was a good idea to contact them and ask about any specific uncomfortable situations in their courses involving military students. Smiley thought it was a great idea; it could help in building a case, but he recommended to ask about all students, not just military students. At this point, Pvt. Stone is a suspect, but she may not be the only one. April let that sink in a second. This is scary. Multiple students were involved in the cheating ring that they broke up a few months ago.

"It makes one wonder about people," she said. "But I know that there are only a small group of students who cheat, and even less that would go to the extremes of killing someone." April confirmed the office would do what it can to help identify those who might be involved and she would let Det. Smiley know as soon as she had information for him.

April pulled her leadership team together in the "dining room," converted to conference room, to develop a plan for contacting faculty and asking for their support in this investigation. April and Bev Peterson developed the email for the faculty while Bob grabbed Reggie to run a list of all active faculty and write a program to personalize the email message to send it out. With the project under control, April told everybody to call it a day. The message would be sent out in the morning.

What a day this has been. April left the office drained, wanting to get home and unwind for a while.

It has been a long day, thought April. *I am so tired.* The past few days have just been crazy.

"I need to relax and baking something will do the trick. I have always found baking to be relaxing and the office staff don't seem to mind eating the baked goods. I've been so busy that I haven't baked; the staff are going to be happy. I'll make a favorite, pecan pie bars. It's my friend Susan's recipe and I am sure glad she shared it with me. I like to get my hands into my baking and with this recipe I can do that."

April started with flour, confectioner's sugar, and cold butter. She cuts the butter in with her hands. Working up the dough helps relieve the stress of the day. April spreads the dough in the baking dish and places it in the oven. While it bakes for ten minutes, she cleans the bowl to make the topping. April beats one egg then adds a can of sweetened condensed milk, Heath brickle chips, and finely chopped pecans. She pulls the pan out of the oven and pours the mixture over the crust that has baked for ten minutes. April returns the pan to the oven to bake for twenty-five minutes more. The kitchen started to smell like pecan pie. It's better than lighting a fragrant candle any day. April poured a glass of wine and plopped on the couch.

"I have not had a chance to unwind in days. This whole ordeal is just so unreal. How can Gloria Benson be dead? How can our students be involved? This is so much to take in."

Chapter Fifteen

Meanwhile, Emily had no idea things were starting to unravel for her. Det. Smiley was putting pieces together and was tracking her. Emily was not a hardened criminal and didn't stop to think about using her own credit and bank cards and how they would make it easy for the police to track her. After Det. Smiley had put Emily Stone on his suspect list, he indeed started to track her movements. He had her service record, he had talked Dr. McKenzie about the cheating incident, he had requested her bank statements, credit card charges, and was tracking her charges. He also put in a request for her phone records.

Det. Smiley knew that Emily was from South Dakota and when he reviewed her credit card charges, he could track that she was headed that way. He called her parents; they had not heard from her. Det. Smiley explained he knew the army had contacted them too but wanted to check to see if they had heard anything yet. He had to be careful not to let them know that Emily was a murder suspect. He just mentioned that Birmingham PD was involved as Emily had friends there. It was a little white lie but there was no need to upset them when he wasn't sure yet that Emily murdered Dr. Benson. Emily's mother assured him that they would call him if they heard from her. After explaining the situation to Emily's parents, Smiley felt sure they would contact him if Emily did reach out to her family. Det. Smiley was sure her parents would be putting in a call to her. Little did he know that her parents had been reaching out to her. She wasn't answering knowing the army would have contacted them. Now Emily had decided to dump her phone so she couldn't be tracked through it.

Det. Smiley was doing his daily check of Emily Stone's credit card charges and found something interesting, Emily stayed a couple of nights in Miller, South Dakota. He wondered if she might still be in the area. Time to contact the local police. After a few calls, he found the phone number for the Miller Police. He left his phone number for a callback, leaving a short message this was related to an incident in Birmingham. A few hours later, Smiley had a call from Deputy Shane Anderson from the Hand County Sherriff's Department. The Miller Police Department, thinking this inquiry may be related to the murder, asked Shane to make the return call.

Smiley started, "Thank you for returning my call, Deputy. I have been trying to track down an AWOL soldier from South Dakota who was a person of interest in a murder in Birmingham. An instructor for DTI Online was murdered Saturday night. The perp used a KA-BAR to slit her throat. So far in the investigation, this AWOL Soldier, a student at DTI Online, is a strong person of interest. I have been tracking her credit card charges and she has spent two nights at the Miller Super 8."

Deputy Anderson said, "Oh man, I just got back to the station after being called to a murder near Miller. It appears that the subject had been killed with knife. According to the CSI team and the coroner, possibly a military knife, like a KA-BAR."

After comparing notes, Smiley ended the call by saying, "I'm on the next flight out to Miller."

What Smiley soon found out, he would not be flying directly into Miller, South Dakota.

Chapter Sixteen

Emily rolled into Bolton and realized she didn't know where Haley lived.

"I better pull over and text her." Emily texted Haley from the parking lot: "*Hey, you at home. It's Emily and I'm in Bolton. Had to get a new phone. Can we get together?*"

It was only about five minutes and Haley texted back. "*Wow, you are here. What's up?*"

Emily responded: "*Need to talk. Can I come to your place?*"

Haley texted her address.

Ten minutes later, Emily pulled up at Haley's apartment. Haley's apartment was above an old, abandoned store at the end of Bolton's main street. She pulled her bag out of the car and went up the stairs to the door.

Haley answered the door and exclaimed, "You look like hell!"

Emily responded, "I have a lot to tell you, but first can I take a shower?"

Once she was in the apartment proper, Emily looked around. *What a pigsty,* thought Emily. *I hope the bathroom isn't this bad.*

Haley showed her in then set her up for a shower. Emily was happy the bathroom wasn't as bad as the living room. She stood under the hot water and let it wash the day away.

Meanwhile, Haley's boyfriend, Butch, dropped by. Emily was a little taken back when she came out of the bedroom to see Butch. He was a rather rough-looking dude, like a guy from a biker gang. Emily really wanted to talk to Haley about the past few days and wondered if it be safe to talk in front of this guy.

Haley started out by introducing Butch to Emily. "Butch is a semi-truck mechanic who works at the big truck stop out on 129."

Emily thought, *Maybe first appearances aren't anything to worry about. He seems nice.*

Haley said that they could talk about what happened with DTI Online, she had told him everything. So Emily started spilling everything—how mad she was with Dr. Benson, for ruining her military career, how she hated her. Emily had started harassing Dr. Benson and finally she made the trip to her place and killed her. Haley's mouth dropped open and Butch just chuckled.

Emily went on. "That's not all. Colin Kennedy was next on my shit list and this morning, I killed him."

Haley said, "Whoa, we have a lot to talk about. Let's get something to eat and some beers. This could be a long night."

Emily said, "Fine, just not pizza."

Haley sent Butch out to get burgers and beer.

When Butch left, Emily asked again if it was okay to talk about this in front of Butch. Emily was worried that Butch might turn her in.

Haley put her at ease. "Butch is no angel himself. Nothing really bad but he's no fink."

While they waited for Butch to bring back dinner, Haley told her about how she felt about DTI Online and about big her side business that Emily was part of. Emily never thought there were so many students who were in the same boat as she was, thanks to Haley. They hated some of the same staff and both had some unfinished business.

"I could not believe it when my boss came over to my cube and said the directors wanted to speak with me," said Haley. "I was in total shock when they laid out our whole cheating scheme. I guess we got careless. What really pissed me off was that I was being fired and walked out the door. Dr. McKenzie said to me, cheaters never win. They hadn't found out about my side business. But I knew when my replacement took over, the students would start asking about the same deal and then it would really be over. I made a deal to keep from having criminal charges against me and then came clean. But a lot of students were suspended like you."

"From what I hear, one of the IT guys was randomly checking exam videos and came across your group," said Emily.

"Yeah, that's right, Reggie," said Haley. "He went to Bob Lundgren, the IT director who then went to Dr. McKenzie, that bitch."

"Well, from my end, it started with Dr. Benson and Colin Kennedy," said Emily, "and it was like the stars all aligned to screw us. Colin got into one of our group chats by accident and saw how I was planning to cheat on the biology final with your exam information. He went right to Dr. Benson. Of course, you know what happened from there. Dr. Benson went to Dr. McKenzie then she failed me and it was all part of our downfall, me suspended and you fired. Well, I have had my revenge on both Dr. Benson and Colin. They are both dead. But Reggie is who I am after next, that will make me even."

Butch returned with burgers and fries from the diner and a case of beer. Emily didn't realize how hungry she was for some good food after that really bad pizza and these burgers were great. So was the beer. After a couple, she started to relax. The discussion after dinner went back to the events that led up to Haley being fired and Emily being suspended. They talked about what should be done with Reggie *and* Dr. McKenzie.

Butch, who also had a few beers, said to them both, "You are making my ass hurt, why don't you quit bitching and plan on doing something about it?"

Haley really hates Reggie and Dr. McKenzie. She and Butch had been talking about taking Reggie out. After a few more beers, no one was making sense, so they all decided it was time to crash and start anew tomorrow.

When Emily went to sleep that night, she wondered if she could trust Haley and Butch. It appears she has really gotten in with the wrong people. This is not what she wanted for her life. Maybe she should just turn herself in. It appears that Haley is more of a criminal than she thought and keeping company with the likes of Butch didn't make Emily feel all warm and fuzzy. She thought, *Haley wants to deal with Dr. McKenzie. I don't want to go that far.*

Thursday

Chapter Seventeen

The next morning, Haley came in and woke Emily. Emily couldn't believe how long she had slept, too much stress and too many beers had put Emily right out. Haley had the morning paper; the headline was all about the murder of Colin Kennedy.

Oh, boy, thought Emily, *what am I going to do?*

She started reading the article to see what the police had said. The article described a brutal murder of a well-known and loved member of the Miller area. Colin had a wife and two young children. Emily knew that but now after the fact, she was saddened about Colin being dead. The reporter had interviewed Deputy Shane Anderson of the Hand County Sherriff's Office. Deputy Anderson had described the murder as a violent act and one possibly carried out by someone with military experience.

Oh no! thought Emily. *Maybe they know something.*

Emily told Haley she would shower and be right out. She asked about coffee and Haley told her it was already made.

After a shower and some coffee, Emily started to feel human again, but she was hungry. Haley sent Butch out for some lunch as she wanted to talk to Emily.

"This is serious shit, Emily," started Haley. "You have killed two people. What are you planning to do?"

Emily put her head in her hands for a few seconds and then looked up at Haley. "My life is ruined. It was ruined by that bitch Benson and Colin. I lost any chance of getting into cybersecurity in the army when Benson turned me in for cheating. I had to do something and I just sort of snapped."

"Well, I am in the same boat as you, Emily, I lost my job," snapped Haley.

"I know, I know!" shouted Emily. "Sorry, Haley, I am so stressed out. I don't know what to do other than keep on my path of revenge. There are others I still hold accountable, same as you, Reggie Smith."

Haley added, "And Dr. McKenzie."

"You want to go after them?" asked Haley.

"Yes," said Emily, "I want to get my revenge and then disappear to somewhere where no one will find me. I thought of Arizona or maybe Mexico, but I would have to create a new identity and get forged papers to do that."

About that time, Butch came back with lunch.

"Let's eat," said Haley with a shitty grin on her face. "And then do some planning."

With lunch over, Emily, Haley, and Butch started planning "how to take out" Reggie. Haley knew that Reggie liked to walk along the bluff above the Missouri River during his lunch hour.

"I think it would be very easy to push Reggie right off the bluff," said Haley. "He's the thin, lanky type of guy and it shouldn't take much to push him—to make it look like he fell, an accident."

Butch, who has been quiet through all the discussion, looks at Emily and asked, "What did you do with your KA-BAR?"

Emily, a little taken back, responded, "I got rid of it after I got rid of Colin."

"Oh," said Butch, "I was just wondering, I thought if we had your KA-BAR, it might come in handy if we have trouble with Reggie."

Emily didn't think much about it then, but she should have.

Chapter Eighteen

Det. Smiley managed to get a flight out of Birmingham to Memphis and on to Minneapolis. You don't fly into South Dakota without going to Minneapolis when coming from the east. However, he couldn't get into South Dakota that night. After a long evening on a plane to Minneapolis and a night in the airport for the 6:00 a.m. flight to Sioux Falls, Det. Smiley was driving a rental car to Miller to meet State Deputy Shane Anderson.

Good Lord, thought Smiley, *this state is flat and barren, there are no trees.*

There was plenty of farmland in Alabama but around Birmingham, it was hilly and plush with trees. Also, Smiley couldn't believe the speed limit on I29 was eighty miles per hour. It didn't take long to get to the Brookings exit but that drive along Route 14 was a long one. Finally, just after noon, Smiley arrived at the sheriff's office.

Deputy Anderson came out to meet Det. Smiley.

He took one look at Smiley, who was a little worse for wear after a long night, and said, "Let's go get something to eat, you look like you could use a good meal."

Smiley shook his head yes.

"Let's head over to the Turtle Creek Saloon for a burger, they make the best burgers in town. There is nothing like good western beef."

Smiley wondered if he was actually in the old west.

Deputy Anderson wasn't wrong, thought Det. Smiley as he woofed down his burger with a diet Coke. He and Deputy Anderson had agreed to a first-name basis, Shane and Darius, and after some small talk about the differences between Alabama and South Dakota, they settled into some serious discussion on the case.

Darius was catching Shane up on the murder in Birmingham… "When I reviewed the hate-filled emails from Emily Stone that Mr. Benson brought in, I had a sinking feeling she could be trouble. We, of course, put the Benson home on hourly drive by while Mr. Benson was away. You know how it is, threats are not enough for an arrest and at the time, we didn't believe Pvt. Stone knew where the Bensons lived."

Shane shook his head in response.

Darius continued, "I am having a hard time with this case. I never thought Dr. Benson would die in the manner she did. Her throat was sliced with what we think was a KA-BAR. I need to clear this case. As you know, I followed up with Dr. McKenzie, Director of DTI Online, and that is when I confirmed that Pvt. Stone was part of a cheating scandal and that she blamed Dr. Benson for her being suspended from the program. From there, I confirmed that Pvt. Stone is AWOL and that put her at the top of my suspect list."

Shane commented, "It appears Colin Kennedy was killed in a similar manner. I contacted Julie, his widow, to see if Colin happened to be a student at DTI and he was. In fact, he had taken Dr. Benson's biology course. Julie filled me in on part of this cheating scandal. Colin had gone to Dr. Benson with some suspicions about a student cheating on exams which he had picked up in some online student chat room conversations. We should probably get more insight from Dr. McKenzie."

"That would be a good idea," noted Darius. "Dr. McKenzie sent me some of the file on the situation, but it is always good to get the information firsthand. I can call her to see if she is available this afternoon."

"Good idea," said Shane. "Just keep in mind that is a two-and-a-half-hour drive. Make it 3:30 or later."

Darius thought to himself, *Oh joy, more driving. What is it with this state and how far away each town is?*

Shane continued, "We will stop by the Super 8 and get you a room. It will be late getting back. If you have a photo of Pvt. Stone, we can show it to the registration clerk. She should recognize her since she stayed there."

With that, calls were made, appointments were set, and the two law enforcement officers hit the road.

Chapter Nineteen

One the way to Bolton, Darius and Shane felt pretty good about what they had accomplished so far. For one thing, the Super 8 registration clerk did remember Pvt Stone staying at the motel. She looked up the records confirming Emily arrived there Monday night, checking out Wednesday morning. Shane took Darius down the road past where Colin had been killed so he could see the scene. Colin's truck had not been moved back up to his house yet. Darius could see where Colin bled out. Also, Shane showed him the tire tread that the CSI team had made molds of. It appears another car had been parked there.

Darius and Shane were talking out scenarios to figure out what Emily did to have Colin stop and what would have left him vulnerable. They believe her car was the decoy. Colin stopped for car problems, that had to be it. He got out and went to see what the problem was. He didn't know what was about to happen until it was too late. With that sobering thought, Shane and Darius drove in silence.

As they drew closer to Bolton, Shane started to tell Darius about the institute. Dakota Technical Institute was designated as the state's technology institution but has grown to be a nationally renowned institution for cybersecurity. When online programs were developed to accommodate students from around the country, DTI decided to make use of the asylum property for office space and the administrator's home was renovated to be the home of DTI Online. There are many stories tied to the treatment of the patients at the asylum, but it is a beautiful old building. The university needed to make use of the property. Along with becoming the home of DTI Online, the old asylum itself had been renovated to create a museum in the front part of the building.

As Shane drove through Bolton, Darius could see the institute, but it was the asylum on the bluff that he couldn't stop looking at. It was indeed a beautiful Victorian building, but it was also a little eerie.

Darius thought to himself, *I wouldn't want to be caught up there after dark.*

Shane noticed Darius staring at the building. "Quite a sight, isn't it?" said Shane, which brought Darius back to reality. Shane continued, "That is the Wildflower Asylum. I understand if you were placed in that institution in the early days, you rarely came out. Services improved over time, but the asylum was not kept up. A new facility was opened in Yankton and this place was closed down in the seventies."

Although Det. Darius Smiley was a large and somewhat ominous man, he did a quick shudder and hoped he would never have to go up there.

As Shane pulled onto the road leading to the bluff, he said to Darius, "This is where the DTI Online office is located. The director is Dr. April McKenzie; I have never met her. But you know what those academic types are like."

Darius shook his head yes. He had to "deal with academic types" at UAB, University of Alabama Birmingham.

The Wildflower Asylum consisted of a huge three-story hospital with a Victorian design. It's a beautiful brick building with huge windows for every room, all covered with wrought iron bars. It gives off an aura of a fancy prison. There are barns, a maintenance building, and boiler room at the back of the grounds. There are beautiful gardens around the hospital and the administrator's home. The administrator's home is a smaller version of the hospital, a brick Victorian home but without the bars on the windows. This beautiful building is the home of DTI Online. The huge dining room is the conference room, with huge arched windows and beautiful oak wainscot all around. The parlor is the director's office and the library is the reception area. The bedrooms upstairs, along with the parlor, have fireplaces, which of course, the university doesn't allow the staff to use. The bedrooms have been divided into office cubicles for staff and the pantry has been turned into records storage. The large kitchen is used for a break room and copy room. Over the years, the pipes in the bathrooms and the wirings have been updated for technology needed to operate DTI Online. Fresh paint and office furniture have slowly pulled the building away from its Victorian splendor. The building is not ADA compliant until an elevator is added. However, there are both a grand staircase to the second floor from the entryway and a back staircase from the kitchen to the second floor; not used is the small attic.

When the institute took over the Wildflower Asylum, the hospital building was in very bad shape; many broken windows, peeling paint, dripping faucets, and broken equipment. It looked like a death trap worn down by years of neglect. The state provided a small repair fund so that some of the property could be used, but of course, it was not enough. Over time, the DTI Online office was established, the most critical repairs were completed, and the main hall of the hospital was developed into a museum with a gift shop and café. The museum has been set up to honor the Sioux, as the buildings are on sacred land for the Sioux. It's a small, time capsule in history. The funds raised from the museum help keep the property going.

When Shane and Darius walked in the DTI Online office, they were first greeted by Lori. Lori is a little over middle-aged, gray-haired lady who has been a fixture in DTI Online since it opened. If you want to know anything about anybody, just ask Lori; and she makes great coffee. Her secret is a pinch of baking soda to take away the bitterness.

"How may I help you?" Lori said in her official receptionist voice.

Shane replied, "Hello, I am Deputy Shane Anderson from Hand County. This is Det. Darius Smiley. He called and made an appointment with Dr. April McKenzie."

"Nice to meet you both," replied Lori. "I know she is expecting you. Let me tell her you are here."

A minute later, April walked out of her office. Shane couldn't help but stare. April may be a little overweight, but she is a very stunning-looking redhead. Her auburn hair was shoulder length and it often had a mind of her own. It was thick with some waves and some days, she had to pull it back in a ponytail. Today, her hair was behaving. She had on a hunter-green blouse with brown slacks.

Thinking to himself, *Stop staring, she will think you are weird. But boy, she is beautiful, that red hair. It's going to be hard to concentrate on this meeting.*

April approached the two men with her hand outstretched. She first greeted Darius. "Det. Smiley I presume, so happy to meet you." Then she turned to Shane. "You must be Deputy Anderson. I am so happy you are here to help me with this awful situation."

Shane shook her hand, holding it a second too long. April noticed and smiled. She, too, couldn't help but notice Shane's blonde hair and handsome good looks. It's been a while since April had taken notice of a member of the opposite sex.

He is so handsome and he keeps staring at me, thought April, but she had to let it go and get back to business. April turned to direct them into her office. She looked back. *Oh my, he is still staring at me.* She began to get flushed.

Darius and Shane followed April into her office. April asked if they would like coffee. Both were glad to accept a cup and once Lori brought it, along with some of April's pecan pie bars that were still in the breakroom, they settled in. April shared the history of the asylum. The asylum, built in the 1880s, looked like a majestic Victorian mansion; three stories high with two foreboding towers at each end of the building. At the time it was built, the building was designed to be ornate and pleasing to the eye to help keep patients calm and peaceful. The doctor assisting with the asylum design wanted to keep the more violent and boisterous patients away from the less serious patients so as not to upset them. Thus, the more serious patients would be housed at the back of the building. One wing was for the male patients and the other for the female patients. At the front of the asylum, the first floor was designed with rooms for visiting families, doctors' offices, and the dining room; the second floor was designed with rooms for reading, sewing, games and crafts, and rooms for just resting; the third floor had a great hall which doubled as the church for services. In the back of the building, there were rooms for staff with the kitchen and laundry services. The grounds had beautiful gardens and walking paths, one along the bluff overlooking the river. Since the opening of the asylum, the people of Bolton have also enjoyed the grounds of asylum as well as the patients.

Once the Asylum history was discussed, Shane started right in. "I don't know if you saw the paper this morning, but Colin Kennedy was murdered at the end of his driveway yesterday. He was murdered in the same way Dr. Benson was."

April sat back in her chair, visibly upset. "Why no, I never see the news in the morning, not till the 10:00 p.m. news if I am lucky. Colin was one of our students and involved in this whole mess."

Shane continued, "Colin had a wife and two young children. This has been very sad for the Miller area. It appears we now have two related murders in two states."

Darius added, "I have been in contact with Emily Stone's superior officers and she has been reported AWOL. From some quick checking in Miller since I arrived, it appears that Emily Stone is in South Dakota. We were wondering if you could shed any additional information on the cheating incident and who was involved. We are not sure she is done and she may come here." Darius went on to say he had also been in contact with her family from outside Ramona. They had not heard from her, but Darius was well aware that she is very familiar with South Dakota and would know where to go and not go.

April took in a deep breath. "This is just so overwhelming, I never thought any of our students could do something like this. The cheating is one thing. Some students, although it really is a small group, always look for the easy way to get through their courses and think cheating is the answer. Would you mind if I brought the other directors involved to talk with us? They may also have some good ideas."

And with that, April called in Bob Lundgren and Bev Peterson. Bob is the IT director and Bev is the director of student services. Once introductions were made, they got down to work. Bob filled in Shane and Darius on the discovery of the cheating ring discovered by his staff member, Reggie Smith, and the status of the contact with the faculty about other student disciplinary incidents. April talked about her discussions with Dr. Benson, who reported Emily Stone, thanks to an email from Colin Kennedy. Bev discussed the cheating ring and the dismissal of Haley Jorgenson who had instigated it all. The group made a list of the people here who could possibly be a potential victim. That list had four names—Reggie Smith, Bob Lundgren, Bev Peterson, and April McKenzie.

By then it was going on five o'clock. Shane noticed that Darius was starting to fade a little. Shane mentioned it to the group and Darius agreed, it had been a long day and a long night. April suggested they stay in Bolton. However, Shane said they had gotten Darius a room at the Super 8 in Miller before they left. They would head back to Miller and Shane knew a nice place to stop for dinner on the way back.

"I want to check on the status of the investigation on Colin in the morning," commented Shane. "However, I think then we will come back down for a day or two to see how things play out here. I want to touch base with police here in Bolton and bring them up to speed."

With plans in place, Shane and Darius headed out of the office. But before they left, Shane said, "By the way, I wanted to tell you how much I enjoyed those bars your receptionist brought us. Did you bake them?"

April responded, "Yes, I did. I love to bake. I find it relaxing."

Det. Smiley chimed in, "You can bake for me anytime. That tasted just like a southern pecan pie."

That made April beam.

Bob, Bev, and April sat in her office pondering over what just happened. The three thought the cheating incident was finally behind them and the reputation of the program was bouncing back. Now this was a national murder case. Although the public didn't know what all happened yet, April would have to contact the DTI president about the situation in the morning. However, her more immediate concern was for Reggie, Bob, and Bev. They talked for a few minutes. Bob wasn't worried about himself. He was a hunter and had a concealed carry permit. Although he couldn't carry on campus, he would do so otherwise. Bev said she would fill her husband in on what was happening. Her husband was a farmer and she was sure that he wouldn't let her drive to work again until this was over, he'd be bringing her. The big concern was Reggie. They didn't want to spook him or worry him. Bob said he would talk to him in the morning. Bob and Bev were more worried about April, she lived alone. April assured them she would be okay tonight and would lock up tight when she got home. As April pointed out, Deputy Anderson and Det. Smiley would be back tomorrow and talking to the local police. She would see what they suggest. However, April thought she better mention all this to Dr. Oswald, the president of Dakota Technical Institute. She asked Lori to call and see if he had a few minutes before he went home. Lori told her she could come right over. With that, Bob and Bev left and Lori locked up the building and headed home.

April drove over to the president's office and entered by the side door.

"Hello, April. Come have a seat," said President Oswald. "I haven't seen you much since the Haley Jorgenson affair."

April sat down and replied, "Things have quieted down since then, thank goodness, until now." April drew in a big breath. "We do have a situation now." She went on to explain what has happened over the past few days; how Pvt. Emily Stone had carried out her threat to harm Dr. Benson and now how one of the program's students, Colin Kennedy, has been murdered, apparently by Emily Stone.

President Oswald sat back in his chair and commented, "This indeed is a dire situation and does not bode well for the institute. Trouble does seem to pop up around you, doesn't it, April? I will need to contact the institute legal council and the board of regents." He saw the worried look on April's face and said, "I know it is not your fault. Don't you worry, we will get things straightened out. Just keep me informed of any other developments."

April thanked him and headed out for home with her head spinning.

Chapter Twenty

While the meeting with the DTI Online staff was going on, Haley and Butch were out and about. They went on up to the bluff to take a better look at the path and where the best place would be to push Reggie over the bluff. Butch wanted to make a stop at the pawnshop on the way back to Haley's place. He came back to the car with a small bag containing a KA-BAR. Then one more stop for a case of beer.

Back at Haley's apartment, Emily was nosing around the kitchen to see if she could find something to make for dinner. They have been dining on fast food and Emily was tired of it. She found spaghetti and a jar of marinara sauce in the cupboard. Then Emily rooted through the fridge. She found some lettuce and veggies and a loaf of frozen garlic bread in the freezer. By five thirty, the kitchen was smelling of pasta sauce simmering and garlic bread in the oven. A salad was ready with a vinaigrette that Emily worked up. It wasn't much, and Emily wasn't what she would consider a good cook, but it is not hard to boil pasta, heat up sauce, and bake some frozen garlic bread. While she was at it, she cleaned up the living room. When she was done, she had a big bag of garbage she set out on the back stairs.

About that time, Haley and Butch walked in.

"Boy, that smells good," said Butch.

"Haley, I hope you don't mind that I snooped in your cupboards and fridge. I just thought this would be better than fast food again," Emily responded.

"This is wonderful," noted Haley, "so much better than fast food and I'm famished. And thank you for cleaning up, I'm just not good at that."

After devouring the spaghetti and salad, the trio sat at the table drinking beer and discussing Reggie's demise.

"We found the perfect spot along the trail," noted Haley. "I'm going to stand down by the spot and watch for Reggie, make it look like I'm walking from the other way. Butch will be following him. I'll strike up a conversation with Reggie, find out how things are going back in the office and Butch can walk on up and push him over. We'll be watching either way to see if anyone else is coming."

"It sounds like you have it all worked out," said Emily. But inside she was uneasy, panicky even. As she sat there, half listening to Butch's plans, Emily thought, *Why am I involved with this? Yeah, I want to get even with Reggie. He was a part of all of this, but does he really need to die? He was just doing his job. This is getting out of hand and is overwhelming. I'm not so sure about Butch, Haley even. Now that I am getting to know her and found out what all she did, I am getting scared about all of this. So much for being the tough soldier I thought I was.*

Emily was pulled back into the conversation.

"I said, what do you think, Emily?" said Haley.

"Sorry, I drifted off. I think the beer is getting to me," said Emily. "What did you ask?"

"Geesh, Emily. Pay attention," barked Haley. "We were asking if you wanted in on the action killing Reggie?"

Emily thought for a second. "The more I think about it, it's Dr. McKenzie I'm interested in. You take care of Reggie and then we will plan the next one."

That seemed to satisfy them and Butch and Haley popped open another beer. Emily continued to nurse hers. She was still pissed with Reggie, but this revenge thing was losing its fire in her soul. All she ever wanted was to get into the army's cybersecurity unit and she totally fucked that up.

Emily looked up to see Butch and Haley making out. "I don't want to be a party pooper, but I am heading off to bed." She realized that neither one of them heard her.

Friday

Chapter Twenty-One

Shane met Darius at the Super 8.

"I don't know if you had breakfast, but I was wondering if you wanted to stop off at the diner for breakfast before we head back to Bolton," said Shane.

Darius responded, "That sounds great to me. The coffee isn't bad, but the breakfast leaves a little to be desired. I checked out but what about my car, should I drive also?"

Shane thought a second and suggested, "Why don't we park your rental at the sheriff's office. No need to take two cars, don't you think?"

Darius stopped to think a second. "I think that maybe I should follow you down and have my car handy. You never know what's going to happen. We may need to go two different ways. Besides, I have unlimited mileage."

With that settled, Shane and Darius had a typical South Dakota breakfast loaded with bacon, biscuits, and gravy on the side at the diner and headed back to Bolton.

Driving separately, the drive to Bolton was long and boring. Both Shane and Darius were ready to get out of their cars. Shane had called Darius to suggest that they stop at the coffee shop on Main Street in Bolton to grab a cup of coffee and do some strategizing before they met with the Bolton Police.

After Shane and Darius got coffee and sat at a table near the window, Darius started the discussion.

"After that breakfast, I wasn't sure I'd stay awake for the drive down here. I don't know how you South Dakotans do it, long drives between towns with nothing to look at but flat plains."

Shane just smiles, and said, "You grow up here, you don't think twice about how long it takes to from here to there. Same as when I go out on a call, I do a lot of driving around Hand County. If you drive a lot for your job, it's nothing to have over 150,000 miles on your vehicle in a couple years. Would you believe that you can get your driver's license here at age fourteen?"

Darius just stared at Shane like "are you crazy."

Shane continued, "Many kids are driving before that, helping their folks on the farm. But let's get back to Emily Stone and how we want to deal with Bolton Police."

Darius responded, "I'm sure the Bolton Police are aware of the murders. It's all over your news and that newspaper from Sioux Falls, *The Argus Leader*, we need to bring them up to speed about Emily Stone being a suspect and that she is in South Dakota. I can fill them in on the Birmingham murder and you can fill them in on the Colin Kennedy murder. We need to let them know Emily could be in the area and that DTI Online staff could be in danger."

"Sounds like a plan," said Shane as he gulped down his coffee. "Let's go."

Chapter Twenty-Two

Haley and Butch were nursing big heads with coffee and picking up the conversation from the night before. They knew they had to get their heads clear quickly as it was already ten thirty and they had to be up on the bluff path and in place before Reggie started his lunchtime walk. Emily was sitting in front of their TV, mindlessly watching a talk show, but her thoughts were on what was going to be her next moves. She knew she couldn't leave before Dr. McKenzie was taken care of, but she needed to "get the hell out of Dodge" as soon as it was over. Her plans were to head to Arizona first and see if she can get herself a new identity. If being in the US was too risky, she'd go to Mexico.

"We're leaving," Haley said, breaking Emily's thoughts.

"Okay," said Emily. "Good luck. See you when you get back."

Once Haley and Butch were out the door, Emily knew she needed to be ready to leave on a moment's notice. She thought it was time to get her bag ready to "grab and go." So she took all her dirty clothes and threw them in Haley's washer. She went through her personal items to make sure she had everything she needed to be on the run for a few days until she could find some place to lay low in Arizona. She wondered if she should get cash or gift cards to use. Either way, she had to use her bank card to do that. Emily realized that she wouldn't be able to do that once she wanted to lay low, once she went on the run. When her clothes were in the dryer, Emily went for a Walmart run and to the ATM. She hit the ATM first, getting her daily limit from the ATM and to move some money from savings to checking so she could buy cash gift cards. What she didn't realize was that Det. Smiley was tracking her bank card and he would shortly know she was in Bolton.

Chapter Twenty-Three

Haley and Butch were soon at the spot on the buff path where they decided to confront Reggie. There was a huge bush that Butch could hide behind till Reggie walked past. Then he could follow him until he could see Haley standing at the edge of the curve in the path. She was watching for Reggie to come down the path and she would signal to Butch when she would walk up to Reggie to talk to him. The spot they picked was the stretch of wall where the wall was the shortest. It was the best spot to stop and look over the bluff to the river and would be the easiest for Butch to grab Reggie and throw him over. Both Haley and Butch were on the lookout for other walkers.

Although Bob had a talk with Reggie about the murders that morning and about how Reggie should be conscientious to stay safe, Reggie didn't think his daily walk would be unsafe. Reggie was a creature of habit, sort of OCD. It would just throw him off the rest of the day if he didn't walk before eating his lunch.

As Butch followed Reggie, Butch thought to himself that he definitely looked like an IT guy. Tall and lanky, Reggie just had an awkward walk and he had, what Butch thought, a geeky look. His shirt was buttoned up to the collar and he had a cardigan on that had patches on the elbows. The only thing he couldn't see was if Reggie had a pocket protector in his shirt pocket. Butch backed off a bit for Haley to do her thing with Reggie and pulled out the KA-BAR he picked up at the pawnshop.

Haley slowly started up the path and stopped at the designated spot, looking out over the bluff to the view of the river. As Reggie got closer, Haley looked up at him.

"Well imagine meeting you here, Reggie," said Haley.

Reggie looked at her a little startled. He didn't know Haley well when they were both at DTI Online. Reggie stammered, "Uh, hi. You startled me, didn't expect to see you."

Haley responded, "I have been walking along the bluff path more often, now that I have so much time on my hands…"

Just as Haley said that, Butch grabbed Reggie from behind and thrust the KA-BAR into his chest. Then with one big thrust, pushed Reggie over the wall. They could hear Reggie scream on the way down. The scream rattled the two for a second. Butch took a rag out of his pocket and wiped his prints off the knife and then wrapped it up and threw it over the bluff. The two of them scurried back down the bluff path and to their car. Looking back toward the bluff, they saw a few more walkers but it appeared that no one heard Reggie scream.

Back in the car, Butch said, "What a rush. I never knew killing someone would give me such a rush. I am so amped up."

Haley and Butch stopped off at a local bar on the way back. They were so hyped up and needed a drink.

There, Haley asked, "Why did you stab him with that knife?"

Butch replied, "That was my plan to set up Emily for the murder. She killed the other two with a KA-BAR. I thought I'd use the same type of knife so the cops would think Emily did it."

"You sly fox," responded Haley, "you think of everything." She reached over and planted a big kiss on him.

However, watching him while they sat and drank, Haley saw a change in Butch. It appeared to her that he liked killing Reggie a little too much. Haley wondered if she had created a monster and she wasn't sure she liked that idea.

Emily had gotten back to the apartment and packed her bag to go; she had her Glock and ammo packed in the side compartment. She left her nightshirt on the bed and a few toiletries on the dresser as not to draw attention that she was packed to go.

Haley and Butch burst through the door and Emily could tell they were hyped and could smell that they stopped off at a bar. You cannot hide the smell of whiskey.

Haley, laughing hard, said, "Well, it's done. Wow, what a rush. I was looking right in his eyes when Butch pushed him over the wall," winking at him.

Butch said he had to go take a piss. As he walked past the room where Emily was staying, he noticed how neat the room was and that her bag was sitting on the stand all packed. Butch thought to himself, *These army types, she has everything packed so neatly; neat drives me nuts.*

He never thought she was packed ready to move on.

Chapter Twenty-Four

Darius and Shane walked into the Bolton Police Department and asked the officer at the desk if they could speak with the chief. The duty officer asked if they had an appointment. Shane responded that they didn't but that it had to do with the murder of Colin Kennedy in Hand County. The duty officer called back to the chief to see if he had time to talk with them.

A couple of minutes later, Chief Larson came out to the duty desk. He said, "You want to talk to me about the Kennedy murder up in Hand County. What does that have to do with Bolton?"

Shane jumped in, "That's what we'd like to talk to you about, because it does have to do with Bolton. I'm Deputy Shane Anderson from Hand County and this is Det. Darius Smiley from the Birmingham Police Department. We have a lot of information to discuss with you."

Chief Larson said, "Birmingham, Alabama? Now I really am curious, come on back."

As the chief, Shane, and Darius sat around the chief's office table, Shane asked Darius to start with his case.

Darius sat back in his chair and started. "On Sunday, the department received a call from Todd Benson. He just arrived home from a conference to find his wife dead in bed, blood everywhere. After patrol arrived to find indeed this was a crime scene, the coroner and I was called in. Gloria Benson was in bed with her throat slit. We estimated that it had happened the night before. It was clear the husband was not a suspect. In fact, I discovered that Mr. Benson had contacted the department before he left for his conference and asked for police help. His wife was a biology instructor for an online program from here, DTI Online, and she was receiving very threatening emails from a student."

The chief raised an eyebrow at that comment.

Darius continued. "I made a call on Monday to Dr. April McKenzie to ask about the issue that Mr. Benson mentioned. Among other things she discussed with me was a cheating incident that involved a student, Pvt. Emily Stone, who was threatening Dr. Benson because Dr. Benson had caught her cheating. When the post-mortem informed us that the slit throat most likely came from a KA-BAR, that put Pvt. Stone at the top of the suspect list. I discovered that the army has listed Pvt. Stone as AWOL. Pvt. Stone is from here in South Dakota, but her family has not heard from her. I am tracking her credit card and bank records. We do know that Pvt Stone is in South Dakota."

Deputy Anderson then took over, "As you have probably seen, there was a murder in Hand County on Wednesday morning. Colin Kennedy was a student of DTI Online and in Dr. Benson's biology course. He was also killed in a similar way—with a KA-BAR. Det. Smiley reached out and we found we had similar cases, and it appears a suspect in common. As Det. Smiley stated, we know that Emily Stone is in South Dakota. We have met with Dr. McKenzie at DTI Online along with her leadership staff. We are worried that Pvt. Stone will show up here in Bolton, so we wanted to loop you in on this. It has been a crazy few days trying to figure this situation out."

Chief Larson leaned back in his chair. "Well, you sure have dropped a bombshell on me here, guys. But I am glad that you came in to bring us into the loop. How can we help? Also, have you talked to the DTI campus police? They should be pulled in too."

Shane and Darius wholeheartedly agreed that the campus police should be pulled in too and the three of them started planning strategy for support and was about to call DTI campus police when a call came in from the campus. The campus police wanted assistance from the Bolton Police to find a missing employee, Reggie Smith. Darius looked at Shane and they at the chief. They all headed for the door.

Chapter Twenty-Five

While Haley and Butch were carrying out their plan for Reggie's demise, April McKenzie was busy in her office, waiting for Shane and Det. Smiley to return.

April thought to herself, *It's going to be a looong day! It's not that I don't love my job, I do. When I started working in online education years ago, I knew I found my calling working with adult learners. I was a first-generation college student myself. I was lucky that my parents paid for my undergraduate education. But I completed all my graduate degrees as an adult learner, including completing my doctorate degree online. I understand the adult learners' needs and hurdles. I have had long conversations with students both in my office and when I occasionally teach an online course. It has been my privilege to help students. But this is the day I dread, the day after registration closes. Students have plenty of time to register for the next term courses and receive multiple notices; but for some reason, adult learners cannot meet the registration deadlines and I talk to the disgruntled students who are told no, you cannot get into your course till next term. Let's just say, I don't see people at their best on this day.*

April had just hung up after the fifteenth call of the morning—Joe Dixon. He does this every term and every term, he has one course he didn't register for by the deadline. He waits until his last email from his advisor to say that he needs this course this term to stay on track. Of course, he hasn't registered for it.

Thinking to herself, *Occasionally I give in if the course is in a two-year offering cycle, but today, that was not the case and I said no. Joe was more obnoxious today than usual. I was beat up and I needed a break.*

Lori buzzed to say that Bob needed to see her. *Oh crap,* she thought.

April had been worrying all morning about the murders. She looked at the time. *It's after lunch already,* she thought. *Time sure flies by when you are having fun, not.*

April told Lori to have Bob come on in. Bob had a worried look on his face when he walked into April's office.

"What's up?" asked April.

Bob started, "You know how Reggie takes a walk along the bluff every day when the weather is fairly decent?"

"Yes," responded April.

Bob continued, "Well, Reggie went out to the bluff today for his walk and hasn't come back. I know his habits. He walks first and then eats his lunch. He's a creature of habit, almost a little OCD. I was looking for him at his cube and he wasn't there. On a hunch, I looked in the fridge. His lunch is still there. I know he hasn't come back from his walk. With everything that has happened, I am really worried about him!"

April sat back in her chair, in a real panic. "Oh, Bob, this can't be happening. What are we going to do?"

Bob responded, "Call the campus police on what we suspect and then let's go out on the bluff and look for him."

By the time April, Bob, and some of the staff got out to the bluff path, the campus police had arrived. The group heard sirens coming up the road and soon, the Bolton Police along with both Det. Smiley and Deputy Anderson appeared on the bluff path. Bob proceeded to fill in the group about Reggie's daily habits around his lunch hour. With Reggie's lunch still in the breakroom fridge, Bob knew that Reggie had not returned from his walk along the bluff path. Shane let April and Bob know that he and Darius had met with the Bolton Police before coming to the office. They had filled in the Bolton Police chief on the murders and circumstances so far.

At that point, the DTI Online staff, campus police, and six Bolton PD officers were walking along the bluff path looking for Reggie.

About half an hour after people walked back and forth along the path, calling out for Reggie, one of the Bolton Police officers called out, "I think I've found something."

Shane and Darius ran toward him. The officer was standing near the low brick wall. He pointed out some blood drops on the path and pointed to the face of the wall where there was a smear of blood. At the same time, both Shane and Darius looked over the wall. About one hundred feet down the bluff side lay Reggie Smith.

Dr. McKenzie and Bob hurried the staff back to the office while the Bolton PD took over the crime scene. The Bolton Fire Department rescue team were called in to extricate Reggie's body from the bottom of the bluff. A rescue from the bluff is always tricky. Rope was tied to a nearby tree and one of the firemen strapped up and started to rappel down the side of the bluff. Small rocks gave way as he rappels down. A second fireman gears up and starts down with a stretcher. One of the officers also rappelled down as well to document the scene. When they came back up the bluff, the officer brought up a KA-BAR and a rag in an evidence bag.

Darius looked at Shane and said, "She is here."

At that point, Darius pulled out his phone. He hadn't pulled up the reports on Emily Stone's credit and bank cards. There was activity on both credit card the bank card and it had been right here in Bolton. Darius grabbed Shane, the campus police, and the Bolton Police officers to fill them in on the fact that Pvt. Emily Stone was indeed in Bolton.

Dr. McKenzie and the other directors called the staff together in the conference room to talk about what happened to Reggie. Murder is not common around the Bolton area. The staff was taking this hard. It was a sad day. Many of the staff were in tears and the directors were trying to comfort each of their staff. April needed to contact the president again but this time, he came to her building. As he walked into the conference room, President Oswald demonstrated strength and compassion.

"Ladies and gentlemen, this has been a sad day for DTI. You have lost your friend and the institute has lost a great employee. I know this has been very hard for you," President Oswald commented. He looked over at April and said, "If you can find a few staff, you can handle the calls and electronic communication, please send the rest of the staff home." He looked at the saddened staff and said, "We will be providing grief counseling for any who desired it."

April followed up, "If anyone can handle staying for the rest of the afternoon, I would like a few volunteers to keep serving the students. The rest of you can go home and please seek out the grief counseling tomorrow if it will help."

A few hands went up for volunteers, the first being Lori.

Chapter Twenty-Six

April just wondered around her apartment after she went home. She was trying to work out all the thoughts and feelings she was going through.

Why is this happening? I cannot believe a student would be killing people. They found a KA-BAR, that has to mean it is Emily Stone. Who is going to be next? Where is she? She has to be nearby. Where is she hiding? thought April.

She knew she had to do something to take her mind off what was happening. Of course, April always relaxed herself by doing something in the kitchen, so she set herself to start a batch of peanut butter fudge.

April got her peanut butter fudge recipe from her friend Grace. It is a simple recipe. And it is a favorite of April's friends and family. The recipe is just sugar, milk, peanut butter, and miniature marshmallows. The secret to this creamy fudge is how long you boil the sugar mixture. Since peanut butter makes stiff fudge, you boil the sugar mixture for three minutes rather than the five minutes in most recipes for fudge. By the time April finished the fudge, the constant stirring and then the beating in the miniature marshmallows helped her relax and hadn't thought about Reggie. Just after finishing the kitchen clean up, April's doorbell rang. She jumped ten feet. Catching her breath, she walked toward the door.

Who would be coming here this time of night? thought April as panic started setting in. She stood at her door, which didn't have a peephole and she asked, "Who is it?"

Shane spoke through the door, "April, its Shane Anderson and Det. Smiley."

April breathed a sigh of relief and opened the door.

Shane continued, "I hope you don't mind we stopped by, but I wanted to touch base with you on the investigations so far."

April smiled at Shane and said, "Come on in."

April showed them into the kitchen and asked them to have a seat at the kitchen table then she put the coffee on and cut the fudge; warm fudge is great. Once everyone had a cup of coffee and sampled the fudge, the conversation started in earnest.

Det. Smiley started. "I'm so sorry about Reggie. After our discussion yesterday, we knew that Reggie could be a target, but I had no idea Stone would act so quickly."

Shane then added, "As you know when the Bolton officer checked out the scene, he found a KA-BAR not far from Reggie's body. It was clear there was a stab wound to his chest. So it appears Emily Stone is in the Bolton area. We have to keep closer tabs on you, Bev, and Bob."

April shook her head and added, "I have been stressing all evening about this. It is so hard to comprehend that a student can be doing this."

Det. Smiley, wanting to put April at ease, said, "When people are severely stressed, for all kinds of reasons, can and will act out of character. I have seen murders committed for all kinds of reasons. Some were very bizarre. But in each case, the trigger came from stress from the situation."

April, Shane, and Darius spent some time talking over possible scenarios; how to protect April, was Bev safe under her husband's watchful eye, and how to get Bob to accept protection—he was adamant that he could protect himself. Shane was most worried about April, he was watching her movements while they spoke. He really found her attractive, but he knows he cannot become emotionally involved with someone in a case. April knew he was watching her. It made her tingle inside; it has been a long time since she felt that way.

Darius asked April to go over the circumstances of Emily Stone's suspension again. Darius wondered if they might get an idea of who could be next. April went over how Reggie was reviewing course exam video with an intern and they came across a group of students cheating on an exam.

"What made it worse was that one of the students was an employee of DTI Online, Haley Jorgenson. As we started investigating Haley, we had heard from Dr. Benson that she had discovered that one of her students, Emily Stone, had cheated on her biology exam. It was Colin Kennedy who had come across the chat room communication in the course about the cheating that Emily was involved in. We eventually tied it all together back to Haley's original cheating group and how Haley was adding other students into the cheating ring." Suddenly, April stopped and looked at Shane. "Haley Jorgenson!" said April. "Haley still lives here in town. Is it possible that Emily might have contacted her?"

Det. Flowers added, "She is definitely someone we need to contact tomorrow. Do you have her address?"

April said that she did.

As they finished their plans for the next day, Shane looked at his watch. "Oh, look at the time, sorry we have kept you so late, April."

"Actually, I am so glad you both stopped by. I was freaking out about all this. I enjoyed your company," responded April. She got a warm feeling inside thinking about how Shane was concerned about her.

Chapter Twenty-Seven

Emily, Haley, and Butch were sitting in Haley's living room chowing down on Chinese and drinking beer. It was time to plan how to kill Dr. McKenzie.

Haley started to talk about the Windflower Asylum, "A unique feature of Dakota Technical Institute is that there is a closed mental asylum on the campus. It's a beautiful old building from the late 1800s. The Victorian-style architecture of the building is ominous. DTI Online is located in the administrator's house. The asylum building has an area restored as a museum with asylum artifacts, a room dedicated to the Native American history of the bluff and area, and a gift shop, but most of the rest of the building is in disrepair. It's a perfect place to off someone, but I'm not sure how to draw Dr. McKenzie there."

Haley had Butch drive up to the Asylum Museum before he picked up the Chinese takeout. He walked into the exhibit halls and the gift shop. Butch was looking for any exit that might get them into the old part of the building. There was an exit door for emergencies in the asylum museum, but it led to the outside of the building. Past the gift shop though was a hallway to the restrooms. There was a blocked off door that led to the old treatment rooms. Butch made plans to go back to the museum later to find a way to get into the old asylum.

Butch started, "First, I want to get into that place when it closed to see where that walled off area comes out in the old section of the asylum. I might be able to loosen that up from the other side of that door so I can grab her and pull her in through the door, then I figure I'd take some wire to strangle her and just leave her back there."

Haley said, "The museum closes at five o'clock on Saturday. It should be quiet up there if you went up before dark to snoop around. You might even be able to hide in the men's room until they close and then you can snoop around."

Butch thought about that and said, "You might be right. If I can find a way in back by the bathrooms, maybe I can get that blocked door open and then leave it so that it will easily pry open then I could sneak back there and have you lead her back there so I can grab her."

"Sunday is the least visited day of the week for the museum. It is open 10:00 a.m. to 2:00 p.m. That would be the day to draw Dr. McKenzie up to the museum," noted Haley.

Emily sat listening to the conversation with a knot in her stomach. She knew that she had ruined her career herself and that she had ruined her life by killing Dr. Benson and Colin.

Now Reggie is dead and they want to kill Dr. McKenzie. I don't want to be a part of this anymore, thought Emily.

Emily was drawn back into the conversation when she heard her name mentioned.

Butch was saying, "Emily, who do you think should be the bait to get Dr. McKenzie up to the museum?"

Emily responded, "I'm not sure. What would be the scenario to get her up there?" Thinking quickly. "Haley has the bigger bone to pick with that bitch. She fired her."

Haley chimed in, "Yeah, that's true. She knows I'm still in town."

They each grabbed fortune cookies while they thought about the scenario—what is the best way to draw out Dr. McKenzie? Emily wanted to keep herself out of this murder. But...she thought she might be able to use herself as bait but have Haley do the dirty work.

"You know, they are looking for me, I'm sure. Maybe Haley could draw McKenzie up to the asylum by saying she could tell her where I am, like she is turning me in."

Butch jumped in, "Not a bad idea. Haley could act like she is trying to redeem herself."

"That just might work," responded Haley.

Over the next hour, they talked about how this plan might work. After a few more beers, Haley and Butch headed off to bed.

Emily decided to watch the news before going to bed. She wanted to see what the news had to say about Reggie.

Emily got quite a shock when she saw the report on the Reggie's death. She couldn't believe it when she heard how he was murdered. From what Haley and Butch planned, Emily thought it would look like he accidentally fell at the low wall on the bluff. The reporter said he was stabbed and a KA-BAR was found near the body at the bottom of the bluff.

I can't let them get away with this, Emily thought to herself, *they are trying to frame me for Reggie's death.* Emily now realized that Haley is not a friend. And she was scared.

Emily headed off to bed. Panic was setting in. Emily fully realized that Haley and Butch were trying to frame her and she could not trust them. Emily crawled into bed and cried. Sleep was not going to come easy. She lay there wondering what to do.

I know that I will probably end up in jail, but I have to stop them from killing Dr. McKenzie. I will keep playing along till they go to the museum tomorrow and then I'm out of here, thought Emily. *I'll call and the police and tell them about the plan to kill Dr. McKenzie then head out of town.*

Emily fell into a fitful sleep.

Saturday

Chapter Twenty-Eight

April woke up thinking about Reggie again. Where April grew up, the Bald Eagle Creek (some locals say "crick") flowed past the paper mill where her dad worked and into town where it joined with the Juniata River. She grew up in lush green, rolling mountains which were shaped like the old-fashioned cream drops her grandmother had at her house. When April first moved to the Upper Midwest, she noticed the rivers were no bigger than the creeks back home, except for the Missouri River, where DTI is located on a bluff over its banks. The Missouri River is wide, like the Susquehanna River, as it flows through Harrisburg in Pennsylvania. The Missouri was dammed twenty odd miles west of Bolton. In the hot summer, the river was often low, showing sand banks. But in the spring, when the winter snow melts, the river runs fast and deep. The current will carry you away. April was so glad that Reggie hadn't fallen into the river. With the way it has been raining, they probably wouldn't have found him for days if ever. The Missouri River was high and he would have been washed way down river or he could have been pulled under and hung up on a log. April took another sip of her coffee.

On Monday morning I need to contact Reggie's parents about a memorial with the staff, she thought.

April planned to attend Reggie's funeral but she knew not all of the staff could go so they would like to have an office memorial for him.

April had heard Darius complaining to Shane about how bad the hotel breakfast was, so she had invited them over for breakfast.

April thought to herself, *Come on now, snap out of it. Shane and Darius will be here in half an hour.*

April was working on the batter for her breakfast corn bread when her thoughts drifted. *I need to get this in the oven,* she thought.

April modified her recipe from one she found in a cookbook which she bought at a national conference for online learning professionals. The secret to keeping this corn bread from being dry is the sour cream and the canned cream-style corn. It will still be in the oven when they arrive. April had a rough night and was awake early enough that she could start a pan of sticky buns. She took the sticky buns out of the oven and put the corn bread in. Then April went over to the counter and started cutting fruit. *At least I'll have one healthy alternative.* Once the fruit bowl was ready and April had set the table, she pushed the button to start another pot of coffee. She no sooner started the coffee before there was a knock on the door.

April took a quick peek out the living room window to make sure it was Shane and Darius. It was. She let them in.

Darius said, "Hmm! Hmmm! That smells good."

Shane quickly agreed.

April led them out to the kitchen saying, "We are going to be informal sitting around the kitchen table. Coffee is ready and there are sticky buns, breakfast corn bread, and fresh fruit. Help yourself to the coffee while I check the corn bread."

Shane and Darius grabbed a cup of coffee and sat at the table. Leaving the corn bread in for another minute or so, April put the fruit bowl and sticky buns on the table.

"Take what you'd like, the corn bread is coming right up."

April then set the baked corn bread on the table, leaving the hot pads for serving. Everyone piled food on their plate.

It was quiet while everyone was eating, then Darius broke the ice. "I know that you are very sad about the death of your employee, but we have to get back to figuring out how we find Emily Stone," said Darius. He went on to comment, "I have been a little bothered about how this murder was committed. The first two victims both had their throats slit which makes death happen quickly. This time, the victim was stabbed in the chest which is not necessarily fatal. If Reggie hadn't been thrown over the wall, he may not have died before someone found him. Even though the suspect has military training, throwing the victim over the wall would not have been easy for her. Plus, we found the KA-BAR and it was wiped clean. Was that a sign that the killings are over or is something else going on here?"

That conversation kind of put a damper on April's well-planned breakfast and Shane could see that in April's face. He jumped in, "April, thank you for the lovely breakfast. Darius is ever the hard-working detective. However, we would like you to think about who might be her next victim, Bob or you? Reggie's murder was different from her pattern, as it is. It would appear that Emily has come here and walked right up to Reggie and stick him in the chest. Although we would expect her to possibly show up in Bolton, how would she have known what Reggie looks like or about his habit of walking the bluff path every day during his lunch? We are not sure if she is doing surveillance of the staff and if so, we might be able to catch her if we know who might be next. We don't have staff to cover all of you."

April put down her fork and sat for a minute. *This is so bizarre,* she thought. April cleared her throat. "It's hard to imagine that any of this has happened, that a student would go this far over being suspended. I would have to say that it would probably be Bob, he was Reggie's supervisor and the one he brought the video evidence to. However, you are correct that Emily wouldn't know about Reggie. He discovered Haley's group and Colin discovered Emily's cheating."

Darius jumped in, "It sounds like Bob would be the next potential victim. Seems to make sense. We'll need to talk to him."

Shane agreed.

"I can give you his home phone number and address," said April, "but I can tell you now, he is not going to like it. He will tell you he can take care of himself. That's just the way he is."

With that conversation over, the mood lightened and breakfast continued. Both Shane and Darius helped themselves to seconds of everything.

Shane was eyeing up April. *She is amazing,* he thought.

At one point, April noticed him looking at her, he smiled and she blushed. April quickly got up and offered more coffee. That broke the discussion and Darius said that they had better get going and contact Bob. April wrote down Bob's address and home phone number for them. Darius thanked April for breakfast and when April opened the door for them, Shane touched her hand and thanked her for everything. April felt the electricity of his touch.

April puttered around her kitchen cleaning up the breakfast dishes, but her mind was on Shane. *He is so handsome and thoughtful,* she thought. *At the same time he is so strong and clearly knows what he is doing. But I have a ton of work to catch up on. I am so far behind with all that has been happening. If only I can get Shane off my mind and get to it.*

Chapter Twenty-Nine

Det. Smiley and Deputy Anderson had stopped by to talk to Bob to no avail. Bob, in no uncertain terms, told them he could take care of himself and that they don't need to worry about him. Bob was more concerned that Dr. McKenzie was the one who needed their protection. He felt sure she would be the target over him. She was responsible for Emily Stone's suspension. So with that short visit that quickly ended, Bob, Shane, and Darius decided to head over to the Bolton Police Department to update the chief about Haley Jorgenson.

On their way, Darius took another look at his phone to check on more activity from Emily. She had hit the ATM again and also made a large purchase at Walmart.

Darius told Shane what he just found and said, "I think she is getting ready to make a run for it. But if she's in Bolton, why haven't we seen her car; it's a small town."

Shane responded, "This is a college town. In order to keep parking open, there is a two-hour limit on a space. Emily is most likely moving her car on a regular basis or she has found some place to hide it."

Darius said, "That is what we need to discuss with Bolton PD. Haley Jorgenson needs to be informed. Not sure whether she needs to be told to watch for Emily or whether we'd find Emily is staying with her."

At the Bolton Police Department, there was a group meeting in the conference room with Chief Larson, Det. Colton, a couple officers, and a representative from the campus police.

Det. Smiley was speaking. "Deputy Anderson and I have been discussing the Reggie Smith murder. We know you found a KA-BAR at the scene, which has been Emily Stone's signature weapon.

However, Emily is military trained. She slit the throats of her victims and in the case of Colin Kennedy, she took him down by first slicing the femoral artery of his leg. It would bring him down to make it easier to slit his throat; at the same time, making sure he would bleed out. Reggie's murder doesn't match up with Stone's mode of murder. Reggie was stabbed in the chest. That would not have made it easier for Emily to throw him over the bluff. In fact, if he hadn't been thrown over the bluff, he most likely would have survived the stab wound. Sloppy for Emily Stone. Emily kept her KA-BAR after the other murders. It seems out of place that she would wipe it clean and then throw it over the bluff. We have another theory we'd like to present. We feel that in the case of Reggie Smith, Emily Stone is being framed."

The body language in the room shifted, and the chief asked, "Who would do that?"

Shane jumped in, "We were speaking with Dr. McKenzie this morning, asking her more questions about the cheating scandal her program experienced. Emily Stone was involved in that and it appears to be why she has gone on this killing spree. Emily had been approached about the cheating from a former employee of DTI Online, Haley Jorgenson, who was ultimately fired from her position for being the ringleader of the cheating group. We know that Haley still lives in Bolton. What we are not sure of is if Haley is in danger from Emily Stone or if she is helping Emily. If our theory about framing Emily for Reggie's murder is correct, then the latter is the case. We feel this is the case because Dr. McKenzie told us Emily Stone had no contact with Reggie while she was a student with DTI Online. When Emily Stone was caught in the cheating scandal, she had been turned in to Dr. Benson, her instructor, by Colin Kennedy, a fellow student in the course, both ended up murdered by Emily. Dr. McKenzie ultimately suspended Emily from her program."

This sparked discussion around the table, covering many scenarios. Det. Smiley told the group that he had been tracking Pvt. Stone's bank and credit cards and that indeed, Emily Stone was here in Bolton and had been to Walmart several times. The decision was made to go check on Haley at her apartment. Two Bolton Police officers were sent over to Haley Jorgenson's apartment with instruction to see if Haley had seen or heard from Emily Stone. However, at the same time, they were prepared to possibly find and apprehend Emily Stone if she was by chance staying there. If Emily was there, they were prepared to bring both Emily and Haley in for questioning.

Chapter Thirty

It was a rainy Saturday, a very rainy fall day. The farmers were complaining how they couldn't get their crops harvested, which they wanted to do before the snow started to fly. Usually in South Dakota, it goes from the September "Indian summer" right into snow.

As usual, Butch and Haley slept till noon and watched TV all afternoon. Now Butch was grumbling about having to go out in the rain to go to the museum.

"I'm going to be tracking mud around, trying to find my way out of the old section of that museum," grumbled Butch, "I'll have to make sure I cleanup any tracks I make."

Haley chimed in, "I'm going to come along, I can help you there. We just need to get up there and find someplace to hide out before they close up the museum."

"Well, I have to get the pry bar out of my car when we get there to force that door by the restrooms open," noted Butch.

Emily was just sitting in the living room, nursing her coffee. "So our plan for tomorrow then is for you to call Dr. McKenzie and ask her to meet you at the museum, that you have information about me."

Haley looked over at her, rolling her eyes. "*Yes*, I am!" she said disgustedly.

Emily quickly responded, "Take it easy, will you? You know I'm army and they drill a plan into your head. I wanted to make sure you emphasize that she comes alone. It won't happen if she brings cops along. Just tell her you are concerned about your safety and you'll only talk to her."

"Okay, okay, I get it," chided Haley.

Emily sat back and thought, *Now my plan will be in play.* Emily decided that although she feels remorse for killing Dr. Benson and Colin, she decided she was not ready to spend the rest of her life in jail. She would make a call to the Bolton Police and let them know what Haley and Butch were planning in time for them to save her. *I can still high tail it to Arizona. I will make a clean break and turn my life around for the better. I will make amends for the wrong I have done,* Emily convincingly thought to herself.

Haley and Butch finally headed out to case the museum.

Chapter Thirty-One

Haley and Butch walked in the museum just before 5:00 p.m. Not to look suspicious, they thought they would take a quick walk through the Native American section of the museum. As they entered, the curator reminded them that the museum closed at five thirty. Haley responded by saying that they would keep that in mind. Butch was not at all interested in the Native American section; however, one display caught his attention. It was a layout of the old asylum. He and Haley looked at it carefully, trying to figure out how it overlaid with the museum. It was clear the museum, gift shop, and restrooms took up the space that was the original entry and the hall that was used for visitors, along with the individual visiting rooms. The restrooms should have a long hallway past them that went back to the dining room. If they could get back there, it would be perfect. Haley and Butch headed back to the restrooms to wait. Hopefully, no one would check them.

Shortly after Haley got into a stall, her phone vibrated. It was Butch.

"What's up?" asked Haley.

"I'm going to go through the ceiling tile to work my way back to the old part of the building. I wanted to let you know. You hide out in a stall until everyone has gone and come out into the hallway by that old door. Wait for me there. If I can't get through it, I'll give you a call," responded Butch.

"Okay, but don't take too long. This place is kind of creepy," said Haley.

She no sooner hung up and hid herself in the stall until the door opened. "Anyone in here, we are about to close," said the gift shop attendant. With no response, the lights went out.

Oh crap, thought Haley as she dug her phone out of her pocket and turned on the flashlight. She worked her way over to the door to listen for the staff to leave.

Meanwhile, Butch had carefully made his way across the ceiling trusses with his little Maglite in his mouth. Once he judged about how far he should go, he looked for a way down. Butch ran out of ceiling tiles, so he figured he was past the museum area. He felt down below him, it was plastered ceiling. Butch thought it would take forever to bust through the ceiling with his crowbar, so he repositioned himself and used his foot to kick through the ceiling. Once he had a hole big enough, he lowered himself down and jumped to the floor. Butch knew right away he was in the old sector of the asylum. He scanned his Maglite around to see dust and junk on the floor and old furniture scattered in the hallway. As he oriented himself, Butch looked for the locked door. It wasn't but a few feet away. He knocked on the door and Haley knocked back. He hollered through the door that he would work on getting the door open.

Butch shined his Maglite over the door to see how it might be sealed. Apparently, it was only bolted by the doorknob. Butch had brought a small screwdriver which he pulled out of his pocket and with his Maglite in his mouth, he started to unscrew and take off the hasp. The door had swelled up over time but with blood and sweat (Butch banged up his hand), he forced the door open with the crowbar. He pushed to get the door open enough to get himself out. Haley was standing there using her phone as a flashlight.

She was none too happy. "I should have brought a flashlight too."

Butch started, "I need to go into the bathroom and get some soap to see I can make the door hinges open easier and more quietly. Then I need to clean up around the door, so it doesn't look like it has been disturbed. Hate the early sunsets now. We definitely could have used more light."

Ten minutes later, and with a fading Maglite, Butch had the door where he wanted it and the mess cleaned up.

"Now to find a way out," he said.

As they wandered back to the main door, Butch scanned the surrounding walls for a security system. He didn't see one.

"Trusting souls around here with all the gift shop merchandise," he muttered, but in the back of his mind he thought, *That's for another day.* "Let's try pushing on the door bar and see what happens," Butch suggested.

The door opened. Haley and Butch quickly exited. Butch let the door shut and then he tried to open it again. It was locked.

The door must be locked from the outside, thought Butch.

Haley and Butch hurried back to their car and out of the parking lot.

Chapter Thirty-Two

While Haley and Butch were at the museum, Emily heard a knock at Haley's door.

Then the announcement, "This is the Bolton Police. Are you in there, Miss Jorgenson?"

Then more knocking; Emily thought it seemed like an eternity. Finally, it stopped. Emily was panic-stricken; the police have figured out that Haley is involved. Emily knew that she had to leave tomorrow for sure.

Haley and Butch arrived shortly after the police left. They came in bearing subs and chips for dinner. Emily was upset.

"What's the matter with you?" quizzed Haley.

"The police were just here knocking on your door. They've figured out you might be involved," Emily said in a panic.

"Just calm down," snapped Haley. "If they do come back, I'll tell them I haven't seen you."

"Okay, okay!" responded Emily. But in the back of her mind, Emily wasn't sure she could trust Haley.

Butch and Haley chowed down on their dinner, but Emily just picked at hers half-heartedly. She just wanted to get this over with and get out of here. Butch was recapping how he crawled through the ceiling and got the door opened. Then Haley talked about how Butch will get behind the door and when he was ready, she would lead Dr. McKenzie over by the door so Butch can grab her and pull her back behind the door to strangle her and leave her there to rot.

Emily thought she better get back into the conversation. "Well that sounds like a good plan and that bitch deserves it."

"Yeah, damn straight," Haley joined in. "She took us both down."

With that, Haley and Butch headed into the living room to watch TV. Emily cleaned up the dishes. Then she headed to her room. Butch looked back at her. He wondered what she does back in that room. She goes in for a short time and then comes back out. Emily was double checking her bag and putting out what she needs to dress and get out of there when Haley and Butch leaves to go after Dr. McKenzie.

Butch thought to himself, *I better check her bag again.*

Emily came out announcing she was going to take a shower. After she got into the bathroom, Butch took that as an opportunity to go in and check her bag. He didn't want to disturb anything as he knew how anal Emily was about how her bag was packed. He thought it was odd that her bag was packed to go all the time, but Emily explained that the army trained you to be ready to go at a moment's notice. Butch moved a few items on top but didn't go any further. He did, however, run his hand down the side over the side pocket. He felt the Glock.

Wait a minute, what is this? thought Butch. He opened the side pocket, reached in, and pulled out the Glock. *Emily is holding out on us,* he thought as he stuffed the pistol in the back of his waistband. He zipped up the side pocket and quickly headed to their room, where he hid the Glock, hoping Emily wouldn't notice it was gone. *I now have another opportunity to frame Emily for murder. I won't strangle the bitch McKenzie, but will shoot her instead,* thought Butch and he put the finishing touches on his plan for tomorrow.

The rest of the evening just rambled on and when Emily said she was heading to bed, she was excited that it was going to be her last night here. Tonight, she easily drifted off to sleep.

*The following
Sunday*

Chapter Thirty-Three

Emily woke early. She hadn't slept well again even though she went right to sleep last night, and she just wanted to get the hell out of Bolton. She has had enough of all of this—of Haley, of Butch, and of murdering people. She got up and started some coffee. She dressed and settled in with some coffee. As she turned on the TV, Haley and Butch started to stir. Emily wanted out of this apartment. She knew she had to wait until the murder plan was in play and they left the apartment. However, she did volunteer to run for doughnuts for breakfast which would get her out for a bit. So she headed out to Casey's for doughnuts. Emily was keeping a closer look out for the cops now. She didn't want to get picked up now. She wanted to get the doughnuts and get her car back into the parking place she found that kept her car hidden.

Over coffee and doughnuts, Haley and Butch discussed again their plans for disposing of Dr. McKenzie.

Emily thought to herself, *Quit discussing this and just go do it.*

Haley noticed the look on Emily's face and asked, "Is something wrong?"

Emily quickly answered, "Oh, I didn't sleep well last night. I have a crick in my neck. I'm used to working out every day and I'm just minding the lack of a run or a workout."

Haley just laughed. "If I would exercise, I would feel that way, not from a lack of exercise."

That lightened the mood and seemed to relieve the tension that had been looming over the three of them. Conversation stayed light while they waited for Haley to make the call to Dr. McKenzie.

The atmosphere was quiet in the apartment, but it only masked the mood of Emily who wanted out of there and the mood of Butch, who was more than eager to commit a murder. He was getting off on this and on framing Emily.

Chapter Thirty-Four

April woke up feeling refreshed for a change. She had a nice dream about Shane and felt a little "school girlish" about it. April thought to herself that a lazy Sunday would be just perfect after all that is going on right now. Little did she know that this was going to be anything but a lazy Sunday. April went to her door to get her Sunday paper. One of things she liked about Sunday morning was to have coffee and read the paper in her pajamas while watching *CBS Sunday Morning*. While she settled in with her coffee and some leftover breakfast corn bread, April opened the paper, bringing her right back to all the ugliness that had been going on in her life. Murder is big time in Bolton and on the front page was a big story on the murders of Colin Kennedy and Reggie Smith.

This has been so stressful, thought April, *but I just have to put it out of my mind for a while.* So April put down the news section of the paper and pulled out the comics. *That should make me relax.*

An hour later, after a couple cups of coffee and *CBS Sunday Morning*, April was relaxed and decided to take a shower and go for a walk. When she was done and ready to head out the door, the phone rang. April jumped; she has been so jumpy lately. When she answered the phone, it was someone she didn't expect to hear from.

"Dr. McKenzie?"

"Yes, this is Dr. McKenzie," responded April.

"Well, this is Haley Jorgenson."

April took a deep breath. "What can I do for you, Haley?"

Haley responded, "It's more like what I can do for you. I can give you Emily Stone."

"You can what?" gasped April.

"I can give you Emily Stone," repeated Haley, "I want to meet you but no cops."

"Why no cops?" April jumped in.

"Take it easy, Dr. McKenzie, take it easy," continued Haley, "Emily has been staying with me and frankly, I'm a little scared of her. I can't stay on the phone long. I'd like to meet you at the asylum at eleven o'clock and no cops. I'm hoping I can get out of the apartment and to the museum without Emily. If I don't, I don't want cops there. It could go bad quickly. Let's meet inside in the hallway by the restrooms. If you see Emily with me, just walk on out and I will try to catch up with you again. If I am alone, we can talk about how to best get Emily turned over to the police. Sound like a plan?"

"Well, I guess so," replied April.

"Great, see you then," Haley said as she clicked off.

"What the hell just happened?" April asked herself. "Some of that made sense but I'm not sure I can trust Haley. But I will go and be prepared to call 911 if anything goes wrong."

April sat down to clock watch until close to eleven o'clock to head up to the museum.

Chapter Thirty-Five

Emily heard Haley make the call to Dr. McKenzie. She started to get a knot in her stomach. Then her old mindset on the situation set in.

Why the hell should I care if something happens to the bitch, she kicked me out of the program and ruined my life, thought Emily. She took a deep breath, feeling only somewhat satisfied. However, she had more immediate concerns. She just needed to play along until Haley and Butch left the apartment and she could leave all of this behind and go create a new life for herself. *Why should I worry about Dr. McKenzie; Butch plans to strangle her and that will clearly not put suspicion on me.*

Butch and Haley came into the living room looking like they were all set to leave.

"We are going to head out," Haley said to Emily, "then we are going to party, big-time."

"That sounds good," said Emily. "You make sure that bitch is dead."

Butch looked right at her and said, "Damn straight, we will."

That look just went straight through her; she hated Butch and he hated her. He had clearly tried to frame her for Reggie's murder.

Out the door they went. Emily breathed a sigh of relief. Her life can start again. She'd give them a few minutes to get in the car and head to the museum. Emily went into the bedroom for her bag. As always, she checked it out.

"Oh my god," gasped Emily, "my Glock is gone. That son of a bitch Butch. He took it. I knew I couldn't trust him. He's going to try and pin this murder on me too." Emily took a breath. "That pistol cannot be tracked back to me, I got that without registering it. The guy at the pawnshop was happy to take some extra cash to 'keep it under the table.' Still, Butch pisses me off. God, I hate him."

Emily closed the apartment door and hurried down to her car. She started it up and pulled out of the parking place. She just felt a weight lifting as she drove out of town. By the time Emily got close to the bridge on Rt. 19, which would take her to Nebraska, she felt a pang in her heart.

"I just can't let them kill Dr. McKenzie."

Emily pulled off the road and looked up the Bolton Police Department phone number. Emily's hand shook a little as she dialed the number.

"Bolton Police Department; how may I help you?" answered the duty officer.

"Look, someone is about to murder Dr. April McKenzie at the asylum museum. You'd better hurry, they are probably already there," Emily said, and then she hung up. *That should do it*, she thought to herself and she drove across the bridge into Nebraska.

The duty officer looked up. There was a small group in front of her, including Deputy Anderson and Det. Smiley.

"Someone just called in to say that a Dr. April McKenzie is just about to be murdered at the asylum museum. Who is Dr. April McKenzie?" asked the duty officer.

As she was finishing, Shane was rushing out the door.

Det. Smiley answered as he watched Shane run out, "She is the head of DTI Online involved in the recent murders. We better get up there."

With that, Bolton officers headed out to their cars, taking Det. Smiley with them.

Chapter Thirty-Six

Butch and Haley had to rush and get up to the museum before Dr. McKenzie arrived. The door to the museum and gift shop was opened. Haley and Butch hurried in and went straight to the hallway with the restrooms.

Butch looked at Haley. "I am so amped to do this. I've been waiting to get this high again. I never felt anything like this before. You know, Emily gives me the shits. Maybe we should get rid of her too. She knows too much about us. I don't care that she did kill two people. I don't trust her. Those army types are just wound too tight. I mean, look at how neat she is and how she keeps that bag always packed. Let's take care of her when we are done here." Then he gave Haley a quick kiss for luck and she watched for people while he slipped behind the door to the old asylum. He left it open, just a crack, so he could keep an eye out for Dr. McKenzie.

Haley turned around and watched for McKenzie. It was only a couple of minutes wait until April walked in the door. Haley spotted her and motioned her over. Haley positioned herself so that Dr. McKenzie would have her back to the old door.

"So," April said, "what is this information you have on Emily Stone that I needed to know? I don't know why you just didn't call the police if you were scared."

That pissed Haley off. April had no idea how much Haley hated her. "Look, you bitch," Haley spat out. April's mouth just dropped open. "*You* have ruined both my life and Emily's," continued Haley, "*You* deserve to die…"

Butch heard Haley yelling at April. He stepped out from behind the door and grabbed her. April let out a scream; Haley jumped forward and slapped her on the face, so hard it jerked April's head. Butch got a good grip on April and pulled her into the old building hallway.

Haley followed him through the doorway shouting, "Kill the bitch!"

Shane burst through the museum's main door just in time to see Haley slip through the door to the old asylum. He pulled his gun and quietly ran to the door, taking a quick peak around the door. Butch had April and was holding a gun to her head. She was crying, saying "Please don't hurt me." Haley was yelling at Butch to shoot her. Shane jumped into the hallway and grabbed Haley. She screamed and Butch turned the gun on Shane. Haley screamed at Butch to shoot him.

Shane was yelling at Butch to put his gun down; as each time he gave the command to Butch to put his gun, he would cock his head to the left. He did that a couple times. Suddenly, April realized what he was doing. Her eyes got big. Shane realized that April knew what he meant.

He knocked Haley to the ground and shouted, "*Now!*"

April leaned away from Butch. Shane fired one round right in the middle of Butch's forehead. Even though she knew what was going to happen, she screamed. Then she felt Butch drop beside her.

Haley also started screaming and started to run toward Butch, only to be tackled by Det. Smiley. He and the Bolton PD had arrived.

Shane ran toward April. She threw her arms around him, crying hard. Shane lifted up her face and kissed her hard. April melted into her arms.

Shane whispered into her ear, "I've been wanting to do that."

She looked up at him and kissed him again.

As the Bolton Police were cuffing Haley, Darius said, "I am too old for this shit," as he picked himself up off the floor.

The whole standoff seemed to go on forever but lasted only a few minutes. The Bolton Police hauled Haley off to the station for questioning and the coroner came for Butch's body. Shane drove April back to the police station to be interviewed too.

Chapter Thirty-Seven

On the way back to the Bolton Police Department, Shane and Darius talked about who should conduct the interviews. Bolton PD was transporting April and Haley separately. Darius said he'd like to handle Haley's interview; he wanted her scoop on Emily Stone.

He continued though, "I'm not so sure you should interview Dr. McKenzie though, it appears you are too close." He smiled.

Shane jumped in, "But if I interview Haley, I may try and strangle her."

"Well, we can't have that happening," noted Darius.

They both agreed that Bolton PD should have officers in there.

Haley was placed in a cell. She had a mixed bag of emotions going on. She was heartbroken that Butch was dead and furious that Dr. McKenzie was still alive. She was putting it together, clearly Emily ratted them out and she wanted her dead. Also, it is clear that cop who shot Butch had feelings for Dr. McKenzie. Haley would like to shoot him between the eyes. But she was sitting in a jail cell and she knew her goose was cooked. Haley's only hope was that if she sold out Emily, maybe she would live.

April was first escorted to the restroom to clean off some blood on her face, the clothes could be taken care of later. A female office accompanied her. Then she was escorted to the conference room. April sat in the conference room wondering what the hell just happened today. She realized now that going to meet with Haley on her own was not the best idea. Sometimes, she shouldn't take people at face value. She should have realized that Haley was evil inside and was not afraid of Emily Stone. She had come so close to dying today. But Shane saved her and he *did* have feelings for her. He made that clear. Thinking about that kiss calmed her down.

In the chief's office, Shane, Darius, the chief, and Det. Colton discussed strategy. They decided Chief Larson would sit in with Darius and Det. Colton would sit in with Shane.

"We'd better get these interviews started," said Darius, "Emily Stone is still out there."

Chief Larson had Haley Jorgenson brought to an interrogation room. Shane and Det. Colton headed to the conference room.

Shane walked into the conference room and April jumped up and hugged him.

"I know it's unprofessional, but I had to thank you for saving my life today," said April.

Shane blushed a little in front of Det. Colton and said, "We'd like to ask you a few questions about what happened today while it's all fresh in your mind."

"Okay," she said as she sat down.

"First, how did you wind up to the museum?" asked Shane.

"I had a call from Haley," started April, "she told me she had information on Emily Stone; that Emily was staying with her and that she was afraid of her. She wanted me to meet her at the museum. She said she could get away from Emily by saying she was going to the museum to meet a friend. I asked her why she didn't call the police. Haley was emphatic that there should be no police. She didn't want Emily hearing her call the police. She sounded so convincing that I believed her. I guess I made a mistake."

Det. Colton spoke up, "We had sent officers over to Haley's apartment to make sure she was okay. We knew that Emily was in Bolton and had a suspicion that Haley might have connected with Emily. No one answered when we checked. We didn't know for sure if she was there, but clearly, she was. We had a call from someone saying that you were about to be murdered at the museum."

Shane jumped in, "That had to be Emily. It seemed she didn't want to see you dead, but Haley did. We didn't know about her boy-friend. Darius and I had suspicions about Reggie's murder after you said that Emily wouldn't have known Reggie or that he had worked on the course exam cheating. The use of the KA-BAR didn't match the two murders which we are sure Emily committed. It is clear now that Haley and Butch tried to frame Emily for Reggie's murder and quite possible for your murder. Emily didn't want you to die."

April responded strongly, "I did get to see the true Haley when we caught her, not only heading up a cheating ring but also for letting the students she advised pay to have the exam answers. She had no scruples. She made a deal with us so she wouldn't go to jail. It appears jail is where she belongs."

Det. Colton commented, "We are so glad that Haley and Butch weren't successful and that Deputy Anderson was able to get there in time."

"So am I," exclaimed April, "I was never so scared in my life, but Deputy Anderson calmed me down some as I figured out what he wanted me to do. But that gunshot was so loud and close. It's going to take me some time to get over this whole ordeal."

"I'm sure Deputy Anderson will help you get over that." Det. Colton winked.

In the meantime, Haley was singing like a canary in the interview room. From the moment Chief Larson and Det. Smiley walked in the room, Haley was spilling her guts about Emily Stone. She told them about how Emily showed up at her apartment, telling her and Butch about how she killed two people. She and Butch were scared of her.

"Emily killed Reggie, you know," said Haley, "and she planned the murder of Dr. McKenzie and made us do it. She threatened us and then the bitch finked us out."

"Haley, I find that hard to believe," responded Det. Smiley, "you and Butch are not squeaky clean in this situation. Emily may have killed Dr. Benson and Colin Kennedy, but you slipped up trying to frame Emily for Reggie's death." Then he added, "I understand that South Dakota is a death penalty state."

Haley quickly changed her tune. "I know that Emily is heading to Arizona and maybe on to Mexico. I can give you her cell phone number. Will that help keep me from the death penalty?"

Chief Larson was shaking his head. How easily this woman tries to get out of any responsibility. "There will be no guarantees from me," he said, "that will be up to the district attorney."

Haley just put her head in her hands and sobbed. "My life is over."

Det. Smiley agreed, "Yes, it is, but in your best interest, why don't you give me that phone number."

Chapter Thirty-Eight

Emily had driven late into the evening through Nebraska and Kansas. As she was about to come out on I25, her phone rang. She about jumped out of her skin. She hadn't expected her phone to ring. This was Haley's number and Emily expected, if all went the way it should have, her to be in jail. After a couple rings, Emily decided to answer it, maybe it was Haley. She saw then it was Haley's number.

"Hello," Emily said cautiously.

"Emily Stone, I presume," responded Det. Smiley.

"Yes, who's this?" she replied.

Emily saw a place to pull off the road and she did as she was talking. Her hands were beginning to shake.

"This is Det. Darius Smiley of the Birmingham Police Department," started Darius. "I imagine you know why I am calling?"

"This is Haley Jorgenson's phone. How did you get it?"

"You know how I did, you called the Bolton Police," said Darius.

Emily asked, "Is Dr. McKenzie alive?"

"Yes, she is. Thanks to you; however, we need to talk about you and Dr. Benson, and I believe, Colin Kennedy," Darius replied.

Emily burst into tears. She had held this all in for too long. "I'm so sorry," she started. "I was so upset about being suspended and I blamed everyone but myself. I let anger drive me and I lashed out at Dr. Benson and Colin. But I didn't kill Reggie, that was Butch. I threw my KA-BAR in a pit toilet after I killed Colin."

"You did more than lash out, young lady, you murdered them," Darius spat out.

His anger startled and scared Emily. She gasped in the phone and ended the call.

I need time to think, thought Emily.

The phone started ringing again but she ignored it. Finally, it was too much and she threw the phone out the window and drove off.

Emily discovered that she was in Trinidad, Colorado, and she looked for a hotel for the night. She was suddenly exhausted and she couldn't drive anymore. She saw the sign for her usual, the Super 8, so she pulled in there and got a room for the night, paying with one of her cash cards. Before settling in for the night, she went to the nearby convenience store to get a six pack and a bag of junk food.

After settling in her room, Emily popped open a beer and basically chugged it. Then she took a steamy hot shower, crying most of the time she was in it. Emily put on a pair of sweats and a T-shirt then hopped on the bed, opening a bag of chips. She surfed the stations on the TV, ending up on some sitcom. Emily was trying to feel normal, but she was anything but normal.

Emily had a decision to make. She was halfway to Arizona and what she thought would be freedom, but the cops were on to her; should she do the right thing and turn herself in? Emily thought about calling her parents, but she threw the damn phone out the window. She could use the room phone, but what would she say to them, she was a murderer. What would they think about her?

Fuck, she thought, *I have really screwed up my life. I don't know if I can spend the rest of my life jail. I may not even get a chance at that; I can get the death penalty for this.*

Emily just wanted to go numb for a while. She finished the six pack while binge eating and fell asleep watching TV.

The next morning, she was awakened by a knock on the door. "Housekeeping."

Emily opened the door slightly and said, "Give me twenty minutes and I'll be out of here."

While she was getting ready, she decided on Arizona and freedom over turning herself in. She was remorseful for the murders but not enough to spend the rest of her life in a six-by-nine-feet jail cell. She swore to herself she'd make up for her wrongdoing and help people.

Emily drove over to the convenience store to fill up her car and grab coffee and doughnuts. What she didn't know was that she had talked to Det. Smiley long enough the day before for the police to track her location from that phone she threw away. An APB was put out on her car in Kansas, Colorado, and New Mexico. Emily was only fifteen miles from the New Mexico border, but it was a climb up a mountain and back down. The border was at the top of the mountain and a New Mexico state trooper was sitting on the borderline. Emily was trying to stay in the speed limit as to not to draw attention to herself. She never thought about her car and how they could track her that way.

As Emily passed the sign saying she had now entered New Mexico, she saw the state trooper in his car. She sped up ever so slightly to try and distance herself from the trooper. She looked back. "Oh shit!" The trooper's car had pulled out with his lights on.

Emily started to speed up, but the highway was steep and windy. The trooper was closing in on her, full lights and sirens. Emily kept speeding up, trying to get away. She saw the sign that Raton was just a short distance away.

"Maybe I can find a place to lose the trooper there."

Emily thought to herself, *I have made such a mess of things. I just wanted to get off the farm and away from Ramona. Now seeing my folks and relaxing on the farm doesn't sound so bad. I wish I hadn't fought with Mom over joining the army instead of going to college. I could have been home more often to help out on the farm. I just wanted to make a career for myself, working in cybersecurity, but I have screwed it all up so badly. I have killed two people who didn't deserve it. I was caught cheating and that's on me, not on them.*

Suddenly, Emily came back to her present situation and realized there was one last sharp turn before dropping down into Raton.

Emily said to herself, "Fuck it. I don't want to spend the rest of my life in prison." With tears streaming down her face, Emily said her last words, "Mom and Dad, I'm so sorry!"

Emily looked at the sharp turn she was coming up on. Emily didn't make that turn but closed her eyes and took her hands off the steering wheel; she went sailing over the bank and into a stand of pine trees.

The state trooper got stopped just past the turn. He called for EMS. Emily's car was jammed in the trees and a big branch had gone through the windshield. It was clear that Emily had put her hands up to block her face but to no avail, or so the crew at the scene thought. Emily Stone was dead, a branch had gone straight through her mouth. Emily Stone had made her peace and accepted death with open arms.

Epilogue

Six months later…

Clay County wanted a speedy trial for Haley Jorgenson. The small Clay County courthouse was packed every day of the trial. It wasn't a long trial. The district attorney had lots of evidence against Haley and the public defender assigned to her case didn't have much of a defense. Haley was trying to blame Emily Stone for killing Reggie Smith but there was no denying her participation in the attempted murder of Dr. McKenzie. The district attorney put up a good case for the murder of Reggie actually being the work of Butch and Haley. Detective's call with Emily helped with that. Dr. McKenzie testified to the cheating case and firing of Haley and to how Haley and Butch tried to kill her. The jury was out only three hours. Haley Jorgenson was found guilty of first-degree murder in the killing of Reggie Smith and attempted murder of Dr. April McKenzie. She received life in prison without the possibility of parole.

April and Shane became an item. The long-distance relationship was hard, but they made it work. Shane had an unpredictable schedule, so April went to Miller a lot to spend time with Shane. However, the long-distance driving wasn't what either of them wanted. As it turned out, the Bolton PD was looking for another officer; Shane applied for the position. He had been checking in on Julie Kennedy from time to time and knew that she was getting on with her life. He decided he should too and spent a day in Sioux Falls looking at diamond rings. Life was going great for the couple. Shane got the position with the Bolton PD and April said yes.

Det. Darius Smiley was settled back in at the Birmingham PD. There were plenty of cases to keep him busy. He fondly thinks back on his time in South Dakota. What a different world there. He was sad though at the death of Emily Stone. He would have liked a different closure on the Dr. Benson's murder. Even though he was sure she did it, she never admitted it to him when they talked on the phone that last night.

April was in her kitchen, baking as usual, when the phone rang. She hoped it would be Shane, he was working the late shift. She wanted to tell him about her day. But it wasn't Shane on the phone, it was the campus police. The DTI Online offices had been broken into. She was asked if she could come in to check out the damage and see if anything was missing.

April thought to herself, *Things had just gotten back to normal, what now?*

Recipes from the Book

Pecan Pie Bars

2 cups flour
1/2 cup powdered sugar
1 cup cold butter
1 (14 oz) can sweetened condensed milk
1 egg
1 teaspoon vanilla
1 pkg Heath brickle chips
1 cup chopped pecans

Preheat oven to 350°. In medium bowl, combine flour and sugar. Cut in butter until crumbly. Press firmly in 13 x 9 pan. Bake 10 minutes. Meanwhile, in medium bowl, beat egg, add sweetened condensed milk and vanilla. Stir in chips and pecans. Pour over baked crust. Bake another 25 minutes or until golden brown. Cut in bars.

Shoofly Pie

1 unbaked 9-inch pie crust
1 cup boiling water
1 cup molasses
1 teaspoon baking soda

Crumb topping
1 1/2 cup flour
2/3 cup sugar
1 stick of butter
2 teaspoons ground cinnamon
1/2 teaspoon ground ginger
1/4 teaspoon ground cloves

Bring 1 cup of water to a boil and stir in 1 cup of molasses (I use dark full-bodied molasses). Once mixed add teaspoon of baking soda. Use a large saucepan as the baking soda will make the molasses mixture fizz up. Stir well and remove from heat. Crumbs: mix the dry ingredients together. Cut the butter into the dry mixture until crumbly. Cover the bottom of the unbaked pie crust with crumbs, then spoon molasses mixture over the crumbs. Continue to layer crumbs and molasses, saving enough crumbs to cover top of pie. Bake at 350° for 40–45 minutes. Make sure you use a deep pie pan. This mixture often bakes over. This is a wet shoofly pie.

Peanut Butter Fudge

2 cups sugar
1/2 cup milk

Mix and bring to a boil, stirring constantly over medium heat, for 3 minutes. Remove from stove and add 1 1/2 cups peanut butter and about half a bag of miniature marshmallows. Beat until creamy and pour into buttered 9 x 9 pan. Cool and cut into squares. You can use crunchy peanut butter or add nuts if you like.

Breakfast Corn Bread

2 eggs, beaten
1 cup sour cream
1 can cream-style corn
1/2 cup oil
1 cup grated cheddar cheese
1 can mild Rotelle diced tomatoes
3 tablespoons chopped onion
4 oz diced ham
1 box jiffy corn muffin mix

Mix all ingredients except corn muffin mix until combined well. Add muffin mix quickly to sour cream mixture. Pour into a greased 9 x 13 pan and bake at 350° for 45 minutes or until done. Best served warm from oven.

Sticky Buns

1 pkg yeast
1/4 cup warm water
1/4 cup lukewarm milk
1/4 cup sugar
1/2 teaspoon salt
1 egg
1/4 cup shortening
2 1/4 – 2 1/2 cup flour
Easy method you can use 2 loaves of frozen bread, dough, thawed, for 13 x 9 pan.

Filling
2 tablespoons butter melted
1/4 cup sugar
2 teaspoons cinnamon

Sticking bun topping
1/2 cup butter
1/2 to 2/3 cup brown sugar
1/2 cup pecans (optional)

Dissolve yeast in warm water. Stir in warm milk, sugar, salt, egg, shortening, and 1 1/2 cups of the flour. Beat until smooth. Mix in enough remaining flour to make dough easy to handle.

Turn dough onto lightly floured board; knead until smooth and elastic, about 5 minutes. Place is greased bowl; turn greased side up. Cover; let rise in warm place until doubled, about 1 1/2 hours. (Dough is ready if impression remains when touched.)

Punch down dough. Roll dough into rectangle 15 x 9 inches; melt 2 tablespoons butter, spread over the dough. Mix sugar and cinnamon and spread over melted butter. Roll up the dough, pinch edge of roll to seal well. If needed stretch roll to make even. Cut roll into 15 slices.

Place 1/2 cup of melted butter in 13 x 9 pan, cover with brown sugar. (I like lots of sticky toppings, so I often use more butter and brown sugar.) Add pecans if desired. Place the rolls evenly in the pan. Let rise until doubled. Bake at 375⁰ for 25 to 30 minutes. Turn out on a serving tray. Let pan remain a minute or so for sticky topping to drizzle over rolls. Serve while warm.

About the Author

Deb Gearhart combines her love of mysteries and her experience in distance and online education in her first novel, *Cheaters Never Win*. Deb grew up in Central Pennsylvania, but has lived around the country, working at six universities during her career. She draws on her Pennsylvania heritage and her university experiences to spin the story of Dr. April McKenzie. Deb has over thirty-five years of experience in higher education, mostly with distance and online education programs. She was both an administrator and an online instructor. Deb found her passion in life by helping nontraditional students achieve their educational goals.

9 781637 109342